Two hearts, one boat, and a race against time —will love or work win the day?

When workaholic obstetrician Julie decides to join a dragon boat team, she never expected to be so captivated by enigmatic team captain Rae. Dragon boat was supposed to help change up her routine, not blow her entire life out of the water, but now Rae is making her question every decision she's ever made.

Rae has always been a natural caretaker, and seeing Julie's all work-no play approach to life brings out all of their protective tendencies. The unending shifts and emotional toil of working at a busy Toronto hospital isn't sustainable, but no matter how many times Rae points that out, Julie doesn't seem willing to change.

As they train for the biggest regatta of the year, Rae and Julie must decide whether their budding love is worth fighting for, or if they'll let Julie's dedication to her job drive them apart.

DRAGON BOATS & DOCTOR'S NOTES

HUDSON LIN

DRAGON BOATS & DOCTOR'S NOTES

CONTENTS

ONE

JULIE

SHE WAS LATE. Ten minutes and counting. Julie Chan pulled into an empty parking spot at the Leslieville Rowing Club, unbuckled her seatbelt, and shoved open the door.

She grabbed the bag holding a change of clothes from the backseat and turned to sprint toward the clubhouse, only to stop mid-step.

A group of Asian women were running laps around the clubhouse, smiling, laughing, ponytails swishing back and forth. They must be the dragon boat team Julie had agreed to join mid-season, and suddenly she was struck with a wave of insecurity.

What was she doing? She hadn't been in a dragon boat since her university days, which were... many years ago. What made her think she could jump in halfway through the season and manage to keep up with the rest of the team?

It wasn't like she had any extra time she could devote

to training. Her schedule was already full with all the long shifts she pulled at the hospital. Committing to the weekly in-water practices was about all she could get away with.

This was a bad idea. She shouldn't have agreed to do this. She should get back into her car and drive away.

And yet, Julie's sense of responsibility kept her rooted to the spot. She'd said yes, and backing out last minute just wasn't something she ever did.

As she stood in the middle of the parking lot, caught in indecision, one of the runners broke off from the group and waved at her. Julie immediately recognized her university friend and dragon boat teammate, Beile. A petite woman, Beile was the drummer on the team, sitting at the front of the boat, making sure all the paddlers worked as one unit.

"Julie! Over here!" Beile jogged over to her, wearing a white visor to shade her eyes.

A reluctant sense of relief flooded through Julie at the decision being taken out of her hands. She had no choice now, she had to go through with this, even as doubt lingered in her mind.

"You made it!" Beile pulled her into a hug.

"Yeah, sorry I'm late. The last baby took a bit of coaxing to get out." She offered Beile a sheepish smile.

Beile shook her head. "I still can't believe you deliver babies for a living. That's wild."

Following Beile down to the clubhouse, Julie shrugged at the common reaction. Being an obstetrician was a lot less glamorous than people assumed. Most of the time, she was up to her elbows in embryonic fluid and blood.

Beile led her toward the gathered group of Asian women. Most of them were in their twenties and thirties, though a few looked older. They were of all different shapes and sizes, but every single one wore a curious yet suspicious expression that made Julie feel like an outsider who needed to prove herself.

Focused on the stares she got from the rest of the team, Julie didn't notice the person Beile was leading her to. It wasn't until she stood right in front of them that Julie realized her mistake. She didn't need to be worried about the team—*this* was the person she had to impress.

Their feet were planted wide, their tattoo-covered arms crossed over their chest. The sides and backs of their head were buzzed close to the scalp, while the longer hair on top was tied into a mini-bun. Their lips were pressed into a firm, austere line, and their sunglasses had an iridescent coating that made it impossible to see their eyes.

"Rae! This is Julie. The friend I told you about? Julie, this is Rae, our team captain."

"Hi," Julie said, practically croaking in her nervousness. "It's nice to meet you." She extended an awkward hand for a handshake, but Rae didn't immediately reciprocate.

It was probably no more than a second, but it was the longest second in Julie's life. They stood there, motionless, and Julie couldn't tell if they hadn't seen her hand or if they were simply ignoring it. But just as Julie was about to pull her hand back, Rae grasped it, giving it an almost-too-firm squeeze.

"You're late."

The words whipped out, striking Julie across the cheek. Stunned, she couldn't tell if the scolding tone was genuine or supposed to be a joke. "Uh, yeah, I know. I'm sorry. I got held up at work."

"This isn't going to be a regular occurrence, is it?"

Next to Rae, Beile winced and shot Julie an apologetic glance.

Julie felt her cheeks heat with embarrassment. "No! I mean, I don't expect it to be. But sometimes work can be a little unpredictable."

"Julie's a doctor at St. Mitchell's Hospital," Beile jumped in. "In the maternity ward."

Julie cringed at the term. "Actually, we call it the labor and delivery ward these days."

Rae cocked an unimpressed eyebrow. "Right."

"Labor and delivery, of course! So cut her some slack, Rae!" Beile gave Rae a casual bump with her forearm. "She's busy saving lives!"

Rae's lips twisted like they were trying to stop themself from saying something snarky and unpleasant, then sighed. "Go get changed," they said as they turned away from Julie. "We should be in the water already."

Beile took her arm and tugged her away. "Come on. I'll show you where."

They turned toward the clubhouse, and Julie seriously debated whether she should back out of this whole thing before she got any further entrenched.

"Sorry about that," Beile said, holding open the changing room door for Julie. "Rae can be a bit of a hard ass, especially around punctuality. They hate it when people are late. It's the whole respecting other people's time thing and all that."

Guilt threaded through Julie, making her feel even worse than she already did. It wasn't that she tried to be late on purpose, but babies didn't exactly keep to strict schedules. Emergencies happened, and she often got called in even when she wasn't technically on call.

Her worries must have been written across her face because Beile held up her hands as if she was going to block Julie's escape route.

"But don't worry about that!" Beile exclaimed. "I talked to Rae about your job, and they said they were okay with it. I wouldn't have extended the invitation if they weren't."

"Are you sure?" Julie asked, hesitating with her bag in hand.

"Yes! Positive! A thousand percent! You are a life-saver, Julie. You have no idea how hard it is to find a left-handed paddler at this point in the season. If you don't join the team, we'll have to pull out of the rest of the regattas this summer." Beile clasped her hands together in a prayer gesture. "Please?"

Julie sighed, giving into the momentum of the path she'd set herself on. She was already here. The whole team was waiting for her, depending upon her. She would have to walk back out there, standing in front of all those people, and explain why she was letting them down. She couldn't do that.

Julie set her bag on the bench and unzipped it to pull out her workout clothes. Beile sighed, visibly relaxing as she leaned against the row of lockers.

"Rae really isn't as bad as they seem. They take dragon boat a tad too seriously, but they're actually really nice. This is their baby, you know? They started the team and spent years building it up."

Julie nodded as she quickly changed out of her scrubs and into a pair of shorts and a tank top.

"They have a protective streak too. Once you're under their wing, they'll do anything to make sure you're okay. A real caretaker, mother hen type."

That sounded... kind of nice, actually. With her parents having retired back to Hong Kong and all of her extended family there too, Julie had been on her own for a long time. Even when her parents were still around, she couldn't remember the last time someone had gone out of their way to look after her.

Not that she expected Rae to take her under their wing—especially not after that fraught and tension-filled exchange. Julie didn't need to be taken care of. She'd always taken care of herself, and as a doctor, she was responsible for taking care of others.

"Well, I'll do my best to be on time from now on," Julie said, meaning every word.

"That's all we can ask!" Beile spread her arms and held up her hands in a showman-y gesture, then let them drop to her sides. "But seriously. I'm really glad you're here. It's been a long time."

Julie returned her friend's smile and the weight she felt bearing down on her shoulders eased just a fraction. Setting aside the wisdom of committing to this extracurricular activity and whether she'd put herself on the team captain's shit list, Julie was delighted to reconnect with Beile. She'd lost touch with a lot of friends over the years, what with being swamped with med school then residency, and seeing Beile again felt like she was pulling out a part of herself that she'd stuffed into a dusty, long-forgotten storage room.

"Yeah, it has." When Beile pulled her into a hug this time, Julie let herself relax into it, and the physical contact unleashed a dose of happy dopamine chemicals that Julie hadn't had in a very long time.

The boat was already in the water when they made it back outside. Beile helped her pick a paddle from the barrel full of spares, then showed Julie her spot on the boat—right in front of Rae.

Rae sat with their paddle balanced across their knees, head tilted to look up at Julie. They didn't say anything, but Julie could feel the skepticism wafting off of them in waves. How embarrassing would it be if she fell in the water while trying to climb into the boat?

Carefully, Julie set her paddle down on the wooden dock and slowly maneuvered herself into the boat. The weight of Rae's gaze was unmistakable, two pinpoints of appraisal and judgment, boring into her skin.

Clumsy and ungraceful, Julie dropped into the seat,

causing the whole boat to rock gently against the dock. Then she reached out to grab the paddle, holding it tightly so she didn't drop it.

Her heart rate was elevated. Her respiratory rate was fast, and her breaths were shallow. And they hadn't even pushed away from the dock yet.

"Push off!"

Julie jumped at the shout that came from right behind her, then braced herself against the sudden movement of the boat shifting away from the dock. She took a steadying breath, gripping the paddle to settle her nerves.

She could do this. She had to—they were paddling away from land and there was no turning back now.

TWO

RAE

RAE WAS ANNOYED. Annoyed that Fran went on that ridiculous mountain biking trip when she *knew* how risky it would be. Annoyed that their fears had come true when Fran fell off the damn bike and broke her arm. Annoyed at how long it'd taken to find another paddler to fill the empty seat in the boat.

But most of all, Rae was annoyed that Julie had been late to her first practice when they had wanted to give her a rundown before everyone else arrived. And then annoyed that Julie had a good reason for being late—how were they supposed to stay angry at her when she'd been busy saving lives?

It turned out Julie was a pretty decent paddler, though. Rae had been skeptical when Beile suggested approaching her university teammate. Just because someone had been on a dragon boat team who knows how many years ago, didn't mean they were in any shape to pick up a paddle today. Not if the Lavender Dragons had any hope of winning first place at the big Dragon Boat Festival regatta at the end of the season. And after years of coming in second and third, Rae was determined to win.

The first half hour in the boat was a crapshoot. Julie kept knocking her paddle into the boat and getting it tangled up with Rae's. She kept digging it too deep into the water or letting it skip uselessly across the surface. But at about the forty-minute mark, something seemed to click into place. The change was unmistakable.

It was like Julie's body miraculously remembered how to move, how to angle itself, how to push and pull and twist. The paddle became an extension of her arm and suddenly, the boat was slicing through the water more smoothly than it had in weeks.

Rae was begrudgingly impressed.

"Hey, Cap." Beile slipped into the empty seat at the patio table next to Rae. The team had a standing reservation at a nearby restaurant for after-practice drinks. "So, what do you think about Julie?"

Rae shrugged, aiming for nonchalance as if Julie hadn't been the only thing they'd thought about since the moment she'd showed up. "She's fine."

"Uh huh, and?"

Confused, Rae glanced at Beile who was wiggling her eyebrows suggestively. "And what?"

"And *what do you think of her?*" Beile asked again, her intonation undulating up and down with very unsubtle innuendo.

Rae leveled their best warning glare at Beile but that only caused her to grin even wider with glee.

"She's pretty hot, isn't she? Huh? Huh?" Beile nudged Rae with her elbow. "I know for a fact she's single."

Rae rolled their eyes with an exasperated sigh. "I thought you suggested her because she's a good paddler, not because you're trying to matchmake."

Not that Rae was really surprised. Beile was the unapologetic matchmaker on the team, always trying to set folks up on blind dates with randoms. Never mind that she didn't have a partner herself. She claimed it was more fun to mess with other people's love lives than her own. The truth was, Beile's success rate wasn't bad. Her meddling had resulted in almost a handful of happy couples.

This wouldn't be the first time Beile tried to set her sights on Rae, but Rae had always managed to side-step her machinations in the past. Rae should've known Beile hadn't given up on them just yet.

"No reason why I can't do both. Two birds, one stone, and all that." Beile looked much too pleased with herself. "Don't tell me you haven't noticed."

Rae couldn't do that because they very much *had* noticed. Despite some shadows under her eyes, Julie had a naturally fresh-faced look about her. Her skin had that perfect porcelain glow that many women would spend thousands of dollars to achieve. Her hair was thick and shiny, and even though it was pulled up in a ponytail for practice, Rae could tell it would spill around her shoulders like a shimmering black waterfall.

And she had sexy shoulders.

Rae would never admit it out loud to anyone, but they kind of had a thing for shoulders. It was the curve from the top down to the bicep—something about that line always captured Rae's attention and held it. When it was smooth and plump, without any bones jutting out, Rae wanted to sink their teeth into the muscle like it was a succulent fruit.

They hadn't been able to stop staring at Julie's shoulders the entire practice, perfectly framed by the cut of her tank top. Even now, sitting on the opposite end of the table, Rae kept finding their gaze drawn to Julie and her shoulders.

"Ahem."

Rae dragged their gaze away from Julie to find Beile watching them with a knowing look.

"Yes, fine, she's a very attractive woman. So what?"

Beile's eyebrows shot up. "So what? So, you know!"

"No, I don't know. Spell it out for me." Rae lifted their half-empty pint glass and took a long swig.

"Ugh." Beile rolled her eyes. "So, she's single. You're single. She's hot. You're hot. You two should go on a date."

Rae shot her a flat, unimpressed look, hating how everything always got whittled down to such superficial things. "Because we're both single and hot?"

"Yes! I mean, no." Beile sighed. "Cap, I know you. I

know Julie. And I genuinely think you two would be good together."

"I thought you hadn't seen her since university." Rae glowered into their beer.

"I haven't, but that's beside the point. She's a good person with a big heart. Is she a raging workaholic who doesn't know how to take care of herself? Yeah, sure. But that's your type."

Rae turned their scowl onto Beile. "That's not my type. I don't have a type."

Beile put her hand on their shoulder and gave them a solemn look. "My friend, you definitely have a type."

Rae narrowed their eyes accusingly at Beile, then took another swig of their beer to avoid answering. Because Beile was right—Rae did tend to gravitate toward women who needed looking after. And they'd gotten burned more than once because of it.

"Uh, hi."

Rae's head snapped around at the softly spoken words and a little thrill ran through them when they saw who was standing there. They tried to quash the feeling. It didn't mean anything. It was just Beile, planting seeds where they didn't belong.

"Hey, Julie!" Beile exclaimed, a little too enthusiastically.

Rae kicked her under the table, but Beile just smiled wider.

"I wanted to say goodbye. I'm going to head home." Julie spoke mostly to Beile, though she snuck a couple of brief glances in Rae's direction.

"Oh no, already?" Beile pushed back her chair and stood to give Julie a hug.

Julie leaned down to hug her back. "Yeah, I had a long shift at work earlier, so..."

Over Beile's shoulder, Rae caught Julie's eye. She offered them a shy smile, cheeks blushing a light pink, before dropping her gaze to the floor and pulling back from Beile's hug.

She had blushed earlier too, flushing a bright red when Rae called her out for being late. But this gentle glow of color over high cheekbones made Julie even more appealing than she already was.

Rae shifted in their seat as warmth settled in their stomach. Damn Beile and her innuendos and shameless matchmaking.

Julie turned to leave.

"Wait." The word was out of their mouth and hanging in midair before they realized they'd said it.

Both Julie and Beile stared at them—Julie in confusion and Beile in glee.

"I'll, um, walk you out." Rae stood and as they slipped past Beile, they cast her a stern glare.

Beile looked like she was about to squeal in delight.

"I, um, wanted to apologize," Rae said as they escorted Julie through the patio and back into the restaurant. "For what I said at the beginning of practice."

Julie's lips parted in surprise and Rae noted how they looked cherry red, almost like lip gloss, except there was no shine. They wondered whether they'd taste like cherries too. The thought popped into their mind before they could snuff it out.

Rae cleared their throat before continuing. "I was rude, and it was uncalled for. I'm sorry."

"Um, thanks." Julie's eyes kept flitting to Rae, then away, as if she wanted to look directly at them but couldn't. Out of fear or embarrassment or shyness, it was impossible to tell.

Guilt threaded through Rae. They'd been a dick, letting their annoyance get the better of them. Julie deserved the benefit of the doubt, and instead of snapping at her, they should've given her the opportunity to explain.

They slowed to a stop on the sidewalk in front of the restaurant.

"I'm sorry too, for being late. I promise I'll try to be on time from now on." Julie's gaze had settled on a spot just to the right of Rae's face, like she was staring at Rae's ear.

"Thank you," Rae said, hoping today was just a one-off occurrence that wouldn't happen again. "I appreciate that."

An awkward silence descended upon them as they faced each other on the sidewalk. Neither seemed to know how to say goodbye or how to walk away. And all of a sudden, Rae didn't want Julie to leave.

"How are you getting ho—"

"My car's parked that wa—"

They spoke at the same time, then abruptly stopped at the same time. Julie's already pink cheeks deepened in color and the warmth in Rae's stomach grew. They groaned inwardly, cursing Beile. Maybe it was her planting ideas into Rae's mind; maybe it wasn't. Either way, Rae couldn't deny they found Julie attractive. Dangerously so.

Jumping into a relationship with Julie was not a good idea. Not when Julie was new, and Rae wasn't entirely convinced she would stay until the end of the season. There was a lot at stake, and they couldn't afford to drive Julie away with something as complicated as feelings.

Rae shifted uncomfortably on their feet. "You drove?" They pointed in the direction Julie had indicated.

"Yeah." Julie chuckled softly.

"Well, drive safe then."

"Thanks, I will." She slipped past and headed down the street.

Rae watched her go, eyes drawn again to her shoulders, then down to the narrow curve of her waist and the flare of her hips.

Beile was right—Julie was hot. But also off-limits. Rae could see the warning signs from a mile away. Getting involved with Julie would be anything but simple, and Rae didn't need that kind of mess in their life.

THREE

JULIE

JULIE SUPPRESSED a wince as she tried not to hobble into the next patient's room, a trail of residents, interns, and student doctors behind her for rounds. Viola was already waiting for them, the patient's chart in hand. She handed it to Julie with a questioning look in her eyes.

Julie gave her a minute head shake. No, she wasn't really okay, but no, there was nothing Viola could do to help. Julie considered herself a pretty fit person. She ran regularly, both to keep in shape and to de-stress, and her job often consisted of lifting eight-plus pounds of wriggling babies. But it had already been two days since her first dragon boat practice, and Julie was still feeling like she'd been run over by an eighteen-wheeler.

Whenever she moved, every single muscle from her scalp down to the soles of her feet burned like they were on fire. It hurt to stand up, to sit down, to walk. She'd popped a couple of ibuprofens at the beginning of her shift to take the edge off, but she was probably due for another dose.

"Hi, Mona, I'm Doctor Chan. How are you feeling?" Julie asked the patient.

An older woman, Mona was carrying twins after her third round of in vitro fertilization. She looked ragged after a night spent in the hospital, and her expression held more than a little worry. Her arms were wrapped protectively around her belly as if she could physically fend off the threats to her babies.

Mona tried to smile, but it looked more like a grimace. "The headache isn't so bad anymore. But the room still feels like it's spinning."

Julie smiled encouragingly. "We'll see what we can do about that. Do you mind if the medical team discusses possible treatment options for you?"

She eyed the assembled group suspiciously but nodded her consent.

Julie scanned Mona's chart as Viola ran through the symptoms from memory. Headaches, nausea, blurred vision, and pain in the upper right quadrant of her abdomen. Her blood pressure had been high upon intake. Additional tests had shown a low platelet count and excess proteins in her urine, indicating an impaired kidney. The night shift emergency department doctor had diagnosed her with preeclampsia, and since she was at twenty-eight weeks with twins, they'd send her up to labor and delivery for monitoring and potentially a pre-term birth.

"They started her on hydralazine downstairs, five milligrams every twenty minutes, and then the night shift bumped her up to ten milligrams every thirty," Viola said. "Only a minor reduction of hypertension overnight."

That was all consistent with the notes in the patient's chart, and it was what Julie would've done had she been on shift instead of lying on her couch, staring at the ceiling, feeling like a limp noodle.

"Other treatment options?" she asked the medical team crowding the patient's room.

Three residents all started talking at the same time, and Julie didn't bother suppressing a new wince as they tried to speak over each other. "One at a time, please." She pointed to one of the residents. "You, go."

"Switch medications? Labetalol has been shown to be more effective in some cases."

Julie nodded in agreement, glad that the young woman had been keeping up with the latest pharmaceutical developments. "Dosage?"

The resident furrowed her brow for a moment before answering. "Ten milligrams initially?"

Julie lifted an eyebrow at the way the young resident's voice rose at the end of every sentence. She gave her a pointed look. "Is that a question?"

The younger woman's eyes went wide, and she quickly shook her head. "Ten milligrams initially, then twenty milligrams every twenty minutes. Increase dosage if there's no improvement within an hour," she said with more confidence in her voice.

Julie gave her an approving smile, but before she could ask Viola to change up the patient's treatment, one of the mouthier residents cut in.

"Why wouldn't you go straight to a cesarean? Administer corticosteroids to boost the fetuses' lung function, then deliver. Cut out all the trial and error, and go straight to the solution we all know works."

It was a legitimate question, one that the more scalpel-happy surgeons often asked, but that wasn't the way Julie practiced medicine and it sure as heck wasn't how she was going to teach her students. "Why wouldn't we go straight to a cesarean? Anyone?"

Everyone's hand shot up. Julie picked one.

"Well, the babies are only at twenty-eight weeks. That's a little early when it's only one fetus, but with twins, that's even riskier."

"Yes, good. You?" Julie pointed to another hand.

"Surgeries of any kind, including cesareans, are inherently risky. There's no reason to start cutting if there are less invasive options available. We'll need to assess the mother to determine whether a vaginal or cesarean birth is more appropriate."

"Also good. Anyone else?" She pointed to a third hand.

"Delivering doesn't mean the mother and the fetuses are out of danger. The mother can still develop postpartum preeclampsia. And the fetuses are at much higher risk of developmental delays."

"Exactly right. Surgery isn't the answer to everything, and sometimes can be more harmful than good." Julie handed the chart back to Viola. "Switch her to Labetalol, and keep me updated on her progress."

She turned to Mona, whose gaze had darted around the room nervously as Julie and her team spoke above her. "You let us know if any new symptoms pop up. Our goal is to get you through the next few weeks without having to take any drastic measures."

A quick glance around the room told Julie there were no other family members or loved ones tucked away behind all the medical staff. "Do you have anyone staying with you while you're here?"

"I sent my wife home last night, but she should be coming back later this morning."

Julie gave the patient's shoulder a gentle squeeze. "That's great. Give the nurses a call if you need anything, okay?" She motioned to the medical team to file out of the room.

She was almost at the door herself when a voice filtered through the people in front of her.

"Excuse me, where can I find room fifteen-oh-five?" The timbre of the voice caught Julie's attention, and she peered in between heads to spot the top of a giant flower arrangement.

"That direction," someone said.

As the bodies in front of her cleared out of the way, Julie caught sight of a sleeve of colorful flower tattoos. "Rae?"

The flower arrangement stopped and turned around, then shifted to the side to reveal half a face. "Julie?"

Julie couldn't believe her eyes. Rae was like a vision

appearing out of thin air, so unexpected at the hospital that Julie thought for a split second she was hallucinating.

"What are you doing here?" Surprise made her question come out harsher than she'd intended. "Sorry, I didn't mean it like that."

Rae's lips curled into a smile that made Julie's stomach flutter and her skin tingle. Their eyes danced with amusement and something more, and Julie found she couldn't quite maintain eye contact.

"That's okay," Rae said with a chuckle. "I'm just here to deliver flowers." They hefted the arrangement in their arms. "Actually, I wondered if I might bump into you here."

"Yeah, I work here. I mean, you know that, obviously." Her cheeks warmed as she remembered she was in fact in the middle of rounds and half of the ward's staff was standing behind her, watching the entire interaction. "Sorry, I..." She gestured vaguely to her team.

Rae smiled understandingly, and the expression made Julie heat even more. "No worries. You go. I can find the room."

"Um..." Even with Rae's concession and all eyes on her, Julie couldn't make herself turn away. "Can you find me before you go? Just, you know, to say goodbye?"

"Yeah, sure." Rae gave her one last dazzling smile and started down the hall to room fifteen-oh-five.

Julie watched them go, waiting for her cheeks to cool a few degrees before turning to face her staff. When she finally did, they all wisely adverted their gazes and headed toward the next room.

Viola lingered behind, giving Julie a look that meant she would be getting interrogated later.

There were only two patients left to see in rounds, thank goodness, but Julie had a hard time focusing when she knew Rae was floating around somewhere in her hospital. It was annoying, actually, how much Rae was getting to her. Rae might've been intimidating out on the water, but they were in her hospital now. This was Julie's home turf, and she was supposed to be in control and in charge around here. Instead, she felt off-kilter and disoriented, like the floor under her feet wasn't as flat and solid as it had been just moments before.

When rounds were finally done, Julie found Rae at the nurses' station, chatting with Viola. They straightened from where they were leaning against the counter as she approached.

Without the giant flower arrangement to obscure the view, Julie noticed the logo for The Flower Shoppe on the front of Rae's forest green t-shirt. The hems of the sleeves were rolled up a couple times, and the shirt was tucked into a pair of well-worn cargo pants. Their black leather belt matched the black combat boots on their feet.

The longer hair on the top of Rae's head fell into their face. In what looked like a practiced move, they tossed their head to push the hair back and lifted their gaze to Julie. Their black eyeliner was a little smudged, giving them a grungy, badass look. And when they slid their hands into their pockets—posture straight, shoulders back, feet planted wide—Julie's mouth went dry.

Damn, Rae was far sexier than Julie had remembered from practice, and she felt frumpy and messy in her scrubs, face devoid of makeup, and hair pulled into a messy ponytail.

"The family in room fifteen-ten wants to talk to you," Viola jumped in before Julie could figure out something to say. "And the patient in fifteen-twelve is at eight centimeters, so you should check in with her soon."

"Thanks, Viola," Julie caught Rae's gaze and nodded toward the staff lounge where they could talk in relative privacy. "I, uh, didn't know you delivered flowers," she said when they stepped out of the busy hallway.

"I don't, not usually," Rae explained. "I have a delivery guy, but he got food poisoning, so I'm stepping in for a few days." They watched her with an unwavering gaze that had Julie practically squirming on the spot.

She scrambled for something else to say. "You work at The Flower Shoppe?" Julie pointed at Rae's shirt before she could stop herself from asking a question with such an obvious answer.

Rae chuckled softly, dropping their chin an inch, only to peer up at Julie through darkened lashes. They gave her a smoldering smile. "I own it."

"Oh. That's..." Julie clambered for the right word to convey how impressive that was without sounding condescending. "Really cool." She stifled a groan as her cheeks heated.

Rae's lips twitched like they wanted to laugh out loud. "Thanks."

Julie dropped her gaze to the floor, feeling overly warm from the weight of Rae's scrutiny. Nervously, she reached up to tuck stray strands of hair behind her ears and smoothed her hands down her white doctor's coat. Why was Rae looking at her like that? And why did it make Julie want to squeeze her thighs together to ease the ache growing between her legs?

"I should get back to the store," Rae said without making any move to leave.

Julie nodded. "I've got patients I need to see." She pointed over her shoulder with her thumb, then stuffed her hand into her coat pocket, fingers curling around the pen she kept there.

"I'll see you at the next practice?" Rae asked, and if Julie wasn't mistaken, she thought she heard a note of hopefulness in their voice.

She shifted her gaze from where it'd been pinned to Rae's ear and it collided with Rae's. "I'll try to be on time," she said breathlessly.

Rae waited a beat before answering, staring into Julie's eyes, and in those long moments, it felt like they were the only two people in the building.

"Good." The single word came out in barely a whisper, and yet Julie felt it hit her like a tidal wave.

Air rushed out of her lungs and her heart thudded heavily against her chest. She felt herself swaying forward like her body was being pulled toward Rae's by an outside force she couldn't control. It lasted only a second, and then Rae broke eye contact, turned, and walked out of the room.

Julie poked her head out of the lounge and watched them go, one hand still in their pocket, the other swinging casually by their side. There was a noticeable swagger in their stride, and everyone in the hallway stepped out of their way to let them pass.

It wasn't until Rae disappeared around a corner that Julie let out the breath she hadn't realized she'd been holding.

Out of nowhere, Viola appeared in front of her. "So, Rae, huh?"

Julie stared wide-eyed as her cheeks burned with embarrassment. "Yeah, that was Rae. So?"

"You told me you joined a dragon boat team, but you didn't mention anything about Rae."

Julie pivoted on her heel and started marching down the hall. Undeterred, Viola fell into step next to her. "There's nothing to say."

"Uh huh, nothing except they are smoking hot." Viola's voice was lowered, but Julie couldn't help glancing around to see if anyone was listening. "Don't pretend they're not. I know you find them attractive."

"And how would you know that?" Julie asked defensively.

Viola placed a hand on Julie's shoulder, stopping her in a relatively empty stretch of hallway, and leaned in close. "Because, Doctor Chan, you look a bit like a tomato right now."

Julie covered her face with her hands and groaned.

Viola patted her comfortingly on the back. "Don't worry. Not that many people noticed."

Julie peeked through her fingers to glare at her teasing friend, but Viola just wiggled her eyebrows and sauntered away. Julie dropped her hands with a sigh. She was never going to live that one down.

FOUR

RAE

APPROACHING the front desk of their grandmother's long-term care home, Rae pushed their sunglasses up onto their head and set down the flowers and bag of baked goods they'd brought with them.

"Hey, Amber. How's it going?" They signed the visitor's log, then bent down to pull out a box of egg tarts they'd picked up at the Chinese bakery on the way in. They were still warm, and the delicious fragrance had Rae's mouth watering the entire drive over.

"Good! Ah, are those for me?" The older woman took the box Rae offered her and peeked inside.

"Just a little something for my favorite receptionist." Rae infused their voice with a flirty lilt and flashed Amber a quick wink.

The older woman waved her finger at Rae with a stern look of warning that she ruined as she fought back a smile. "Such a tease, you are. No wonder your PoPo had her hands full with you."

Rae gave her their smoothest smile. "What can I say? I'm just that charming."

"Aiya, get out of here. Your PoPo's in her room." Amber waved them away while prying open the box of egg tarts.

"Thanks, Amber!" Rae headed down the familiar hallway toward their grandmother's room, saying hello to the other residents and staff along the way. After three years of visiting every week—often several times a week— Rae knew pretty much everyone by name.

At the end of the hall, Rae knocked on their grandmother's open door. "PoPo? I'm here."

The woman who had raised Rae had always been petite, barely tall enough to grace their shoulder. But over the years, age had withered away her previously strong and capable body. It was always a bit of a shock to Rae whenever they saw their PoPo like this. In their mind, she was still that dominating force that had swept in and taken control during some of the darkest days of Rae's life. These days, PoPo was still semi-mobile, relying heavily on a walker, but she was much more comfortable in a wheelchair for extended distances.

PoPo had lived with Rae for a while as her health deteriorated. If Rae had had it their way, she would still be living with them. But PoPo had insisted on moving, saying she didn't want to be a burden when Rae was already so busy running the flower shop on their own.

After three years, Rae could admit that PoPo had a better life here than they would've been able to provide. Here, their grandmother had a community and access to around-the-clock care. With Rae, she would've been stuck in the house on her own everyday while Rae was at work.

"My Rae of sunshine." PoPo tapped on the tablet playing some Chinese drama, pausing the show.

Rae went to her, letting her pull them into a hug. They closed their eyes and sighed, missing the tight squeezes their grandmother used to give, but still grateful for the embrace all the same. "I brought flowers and buns."

"Ah, you treat me so good." PoPo patted them on the arm, then sat back as Rae bustled around the room. "You're getting so dark."

Rae rolled their eyes as they filled a vase with water for the flowers they'd brought. "I'm in the middle of dragon boat season, remember? I'm out on the water a lot."

"Ho, you should wear long sleeves when you're out in the sun." The disapproval in PoPo's voice was mild, almost perfunctory, a remnant of the ingrained preference for pale, white complexions in Asian culture.

Rae's complexion was naturally a little dark, the type that tended to tan rather than burn, and PoPo had spent nearly an entire lifetime trying to get Rae to stay out of the sun. It'd never worked, obviously, but that didn't mean PoPo didn't bring it up all the time. It wasn't a malicious thing. It was almost a force of habit. An indication that PoPo cared about Rae's well-being, even if her definition of well-being was a little screwed up.

PoPo would love Julie's complexion.

The errant thought came out of nowhere, and Rae paused as they arranged the tulips in the vase.

Julie with her smooth, porcelain skin. Her tendency to blush left a natural glow across her cheeks. Paired with her round eyes and pouty pink lips, she was exactly the type of Asian beauty that PoPo was fond of... that Rae was fond of too if they were honest with themself.

Running into her at the hospital yesterday hadn't really been a coincidence, and Rae hadn't been entirely upfront about their delivery guy. Yes, he did have food poisoning, but Rae had other people who could have covered for him.

When the order for the maternity ward—no wait, labor and delivery—had come in, Rae had made up some half-baked excuse about needing to stretch their legs so they could make the delivery instead.

They hadn't even known if Julie would be at work, but the gamble had paid off. Seeing Julie in her white doctor's coat, stethoscope hanging around her neck, Rae finally understood why people thought uniforms were so sexy.

Rather than look frumpy, Julie's pink scrubs looked tailored to her body. The fabric stretched snugly across her breasts and hips, making Rae want to peel it all off to explore what was hidden underneath. Strands of hair had fallen out of her ponytail, framing her delicate features, and even the harsh hospital lights somehow made her look luminous.

"Rae?"

They jumped at PoPo's voice. "Huh? What?"

"What are you thinking about?" PoPo asked, voice dripping with amusement.

"Oh, uh, no one. I mean, nothing." Rae busied themself with unpacking the big white box of buns filled with barbecue pork, curried chicken, and tuna. A second box held coconut buns, pineapple buns—which were also made out of coconuts—and more egg tarts. They pulled out a barbecue pork bun and set it on a paper towel before handing it to PoPo.

"No one? Who is this no one?" PoPo took a big bite out of the bun and hummed her approval.

"No one is..." Rae hesitated a moment before sighing. They had never been very good at keeping secrets from PoPo. She just knew them too well. "There's a new team member at dragon boat. She's..."

Rae didn't know what Julie was exactly. She was pretty, of course, and adorably shy. Smart, obviously, since she was a successful doctor. Athletic, too. Each of these characteristics on their own were all fine and good, but combined into the package that was Julie... there was something appealing about her that wouldn't leave Rae alone. She'd stuck in Rae's mind like a burr, and their thoughts drifted to her whenever they had a spare moment. Beile's comments about how they would be good together certainly hadn't helped either.

"She's nice."

PoPo's eyes lit up like she'd won the lottery. "You met a girl!"

"Well, no, not really." Rae lifted a hand in an attempt to temper their grandmother's enthusiasm. Julie was an attractive woman, and yes, Rae was attracted to her. But that didn't mean anything was going to happen. Dragon boat came first. Libido came after.

"When are you bringing her to see me?"

"PoPo! I'm not bringing her to see you! She's just a new teammate—"

"A teammate you have feelings for."

"What? No! I just met her!" Rae bit aggressively into a tuna bun.

"So what? You can have feelings!"

Rae chewed on their bun, sulking. There was no point in arguing with PoPo when she'd latched onto an idea. No matter what Rae said, she'd have a snarky comeback ready, and trying to get Rae to settle down with someone was PoPo's favorite topic to nag them about.

"You're not getting younger, you know," PoPo said, wagging her finger at them. "And neither am I. I want to see you happy!"

"I'm perfectly happy with my life as it is, PoPo," Rae said, feeling like they were a broken record player.

PoPo shook her head. "But you could be happier."

Rae let out a laugh. "You don't know that. Relationships are hard. I'd rather be single than with the wrong person."

PoPo cast them an exasperated look as if Rae was the one being obstinate. "I don't want you to be with the wrong person. I want you to find the right person. Life is long, and it can be lonely. I won't be here forever. I don't want you to be alone."

Rae sobered, shifting uncomfortably in their chair.

They didn't like to think about losing PoPo. She was the only family member Rae had left in the world after their parents had passed when they were a kid. The single most important person in Rae's life, having raised them since they were eleven. Rae didn't know what they would do without PoPo. They couldn't imagine life without PoPo in it—and they didn't want to.

"You're not going anywhere anytime soon," they said in a voice that sounded much too small and fragile for their liking.

PoPo reached over and placed her frail, wrinkled hand on top of Rae's. "No, but why wait?"

Rae could list dozens of reasons, but none of them were really the point. Rae understood what PoPo was saying. It wasn't like they wanted to be single for the rest of their life, but they had never felt the need to rush either.

Rae placed their other hand on top of PoPo's and thought of Julie. Even if Rae didn't need to focus all their attention on dragon boat, it was premature to think Julie might be someone they could build a life with. They hardly knew anything about her. She might not be interested in a relationship. They might be completely incompatible.

"You have so much to give, my Rae," PoPo said. "You deserve to have someone to give it all to. Maybe this new team member is not right for you. But you won't know unless you try."

FIVE

JULIE

"COME ON. MOVE. PLEASE," Julie pleaded with the cars in front of her, each taking their sweet time making a left turn. She was already running late for dragon boat practice, and every second that ticked by ratcheted up her anxiety. All she could think about was the promise she'd made to Rae about trying to be punctual.

By the time the light turned yellow and the cars ahead of her had inched through the intersection, it was too late for Julie to squeeze through too.

"Ugh." She banged her head against the headrest.

She wasn't actually sure how she managed to be late this time—she couldn't even chalk it up to work since she'd come straight from home. In fact, she'd left early to give herself tons of buffer, but she hadn't known about the road closures due to construction. The detour she'd been forced to take had felt like a loop around the entire city. With traffic backed up, she'd spent more time idling in the car than actually driving.

The team was already carrying the boat out to the water when Julie pulled into an empty parking spot and jumped out of her car. She sprinted toward the dock, apologies poised on the tip of her tongue.

"I am *so sorry*," she gushed before Rae could scold her again. "There was construction and traffic and it took me twice as long as I thought it would to get here. I'm really, very sorry."

Wearing their reflective sunglasses again, Rae's expression was as hard as steel. Their lips were flattened into a firm line, and the air of disapproval wafting off them made Julie want to shrink back in mortification.

Julie was a perfectionist. She prided herself in being dependable and responsible, impeccable at anything she put her hand to. She was used to excelling and succeeding, and she hated the feeling of having disappointed Rae.

She had no one else to blame but herself.

Julie held her breath, waiting for Rae to hand down their judgment. She wouldn't object to running extra laps around the clubhouse or staying behind to reorganize all the gear. Whatever it took to win back Rae's favor. She just hoped they wouldn't kick her off the team.

Because she really wanted to be there. Despite her initial reservations about joining the team, being out on the water during that first practice had reminded her how much she'd enjoyed dragon boat. Working as a team, pulling together to achieve a common goal. The physical exertion left her tired, but also with a satisfying sense of accomplishment. The other paddlers were kind, funny, and welcoming. She didn't want to lose all that after having had just a little taste.

Rae made a curt nod toward the barrel holding the spare paddles. "Gear up and get in the boat." They spun on their heel without waiting for Julie's response and strode down the pier.

Julie let out the breath she'd been holding, her sense of relief mild and fleeting. Especially when she spotted Beile and the expression she wore.

"Rae's angry with me, aren't they?" Julie asked as she picked out a suitable paddle for her height.

"They're definitely not happy," Beile confirmed.

"Ugh," Julie groaned. "I swear I left with plenty of time. There's just so much construction on the roads."

Beile shot her a sympathetic look. "Yeah, I know. But don't beat yourself up about it. It's just dragon boat. We'll just, you know, get worked extra hard today because of you." She nudged Julie with her elbow playfully, lips curling into a teasing smile.

Julie winced at Beile's poor attempt at reassurance and hurried down the dock with her head lowered. She was the last person to climb into the boat, and the second she was settled, they pushed away from the dock.

Rae ran them through a series of starting drills, bringing the boat to a standstill in the water, then digging their paddles in as fast and forcefully as they could to get up to racing speed. Julie threw herself into practice, paddling as hard as she could, determined to make up for her tardiness by exhausting herself on the water.

Over and over, they practiced, and the entire time,

Julie could feel twin laser beams locked onto the middle of her back. They bore into her, hotter than the sun, propelling her to work harder, pull harder, leave nothing in the tank.

Her muscles burned from her effort. Sweat poured from her skin. Her clothes were soaked through, and she longed to jump into the water to cool off. She could feel her heart pumping fast and strong in her chest, sending blood *whooshing* past her ears. And her lungs expanded to their full capacity, trying to pull in as much oxygen as physically possible.

When cool-down finally rolled around, Julie wasn't sure she'd be able to climb out of the boat on her own. She couldn't really feel her legs, and she could barely move her arms. Even her mind was a little fuzzy, so preoccupied by the physical exertion.

They lined the boat up along the dock, and Julie winced as she pulled herself up. Her legs were jelly, barely able to keep her upright, and she leaned on her paddle like it was a makeshift cane.

"You okay?" The quietly gruff question came from right beside her, making Julie jump.

She hadn't heard Rae come up behind her, and she tried to stand a little taller so she didn't give herself away. "Uh, yeah, I'm good," she said, her tongue slightly slurring her words.

"You pushed pretty hard today." Rae's tone was slightly accusatory as they stared straight ahead, lips set in a stern line.

But Julie's pride swelled at the fact that Rae had

noticed. The hint of approval neutralized some of the lactic acid built up in her muscles and injected a new burst of energy into her system. "Just wanted to do my best."

Rae hummed an acknowledgment before continuing. "Coming out to drinks?" they said, voice softening just enough to sound hopeful, making Julie pause and blink.

However angry or upset they'd been at the start of practice, it seemed like Julie might have been forgiven. She latched onto that with a yearning that surprised her. She wanted Rae to like her, to think well of her. Perhaps because they were an authority figure of a kind, but also because... there was something about Rae that Julie was drawn to, and despite their rocky start, Julie wanted Rae to feel the same way about her.

But then she remembered where she had to be in an hour. Her stomach sank. She shook her head, and for the first time in her life, wished she didn't have to go to work. "Can't. I have a shift at the hospital."

Rae's response was a slow inhale and a slow exhale, which Julie didn't know how to interpret. Were they disappointed? Annoyed? Resigned? None of those options sat well with Julie.

"We're having a family and friends barbecue next week," Rae said after a moment of tense silence.

It took a second for Julie to remember what Rae was talking about. "Oh yes, Beile mentioned it to me."

"Can you make it?" Rae stopped walking as they asked the question, forcing Julie to turn around and face them. They pushed their sunglasses onto their head, finally revealing their eyes, and Julie couldn't decide if that was better or worse.

Rae's stare was intense and penetrating. As if Rae could see past all of Julie's defenses to who she truly was on the inside. Under Rae's scrutiny, she wasn't an accomplished and highly respected doctor anymore. Her achievements and accolades didn't mean anything. Her stats at the hospital were nothing more than numbers.

Instead, she was a woman who was married to her job, who often had trouble managing her time, who maybe didn't have her shit together as much as everyone else thought.

Julie blinked and stepped back as if that extra foot of space would obscure Rae's vision. She wasn't used to people looking at her like that—like she was a real person full of weaknesses and flaws. Most people only saw the white doctor's coat and the degrees hanging on her wall. So much so that Julie had slipped into that identity until it had become not just a job or even a calling, but who she was.

It was an uncomfortable feeling, knowing that Rae wasn't impressed by her career. But at the same time, it was freeing. If she didn't have to be the successful doctor who always exceeded everyone's expectations, then maybe she didn't need to work so hard all the time. Maybe she could aim a little lower without feeling like a failure. Maybe she could be human and that would still be okay.

She gave Rae a small nod in response to their question. "Yeah, I'll try my best."

SIX

RAE

FLUFFY white clouds floated across a brilliant blue sky and the sun's rays gently warmed everything they touched. The grass, the picnic tables, Rae's face as they turned it upward.

All around them were the joyful sounds of laughter, animated conversations, and screeching children. A group of them were playing tag in the nearby field, and Rae watched the little bodies zoom wildly across the grass. The team's annual friends and family fundraising picnic was always held at Ashbridges Bay Park, with its views out over the blue-green waters of Lake Ontario, and Rae was at their usual spot behind the large barbecue grill.

The party had started about forty minutes ago, but Julie was nowhere to be seen. Rae tried not to let it get to them. This wasn't a mandatory event, and Julie hadn't promised she'd attend. Besides, there were still some latecomers straggling in, so it wasn't like everyone else had been on time.

Still, with every minute that ticked by, Rae felt a little more dejected than they wanted to feel. They shouldn't be so hung up on this one woman. Especially a woman who was busy and had other, more important priorities than Rae's feelings.

"Rae!"

They turned at the sound of their name and a woman with a cast on her arm came jogging up.

"Hey, Fran. How's the arm?"

She lifted the blue cast covered in Sharpie signatures and tried to stick her fingers under the plaster by her elbow. "Itchy as hell. Another three weeks before I can get the damn thing off."

"You're going to have a hell of a tan line," Rae laughed.

"Ugh, don't remind me." Fran rolled her eyes. "Doctor said I'll need some physio to get it up to full strength again. So that'll be another month probably."

Rae winced internally at the thought of being out of commission for so long. "That'll teach you to go mountain biking during dragon boat season."

Fran's smile grew mischievous. "Sasha wants to go skydiving after he recovers from top surgery later this year," she said, referring to her partner.

Rae didn't bother to hide their horrified expression. "Jesus."

"Eh." Fran gave them a light punch on the arm with her casted hand. "We only live once, right?"

"And you'd think you'd try to stay alive." Rae lifted the lid to the barbecue, and a wave of heat wafted out at them, along with the delicious aroma of fatty burger patties.

"Grab that plate for me." Rae nodded to the clean plate sitting next to the barbecue, and Fran held it for them while they piled the patties on top.

"Hey. Julie's here!" Beile jogged up to them, empty plate in hand and a scheming looking in her eye.

Rae forced themself not to react. No spinning around to search the path leading from the parking lot. No grin threatening to split across their face. They focused on adding the next batch of hot dogs and sausages to the grill.

"Julie?" Fran asked. "Is that my replacement?"

"Yup, and Rae's new crush." Beile winked at Fran.

"Ooo…"

"I never said I had a crush on Julie," Rae protested. It was true, they had never admitted it to Beile. And the truth was, they weren't sure what they felt was really a crush either. There were moments—like their short chat on the sidewalk or at the hospital—when it felt like there might be something there. But then Julie would show up late to practice, and Rae would start questioning everything again.

Perhaps it was petty of them to get so worked up over punctuality, but it just rubbed them the wrong way. It wasn't merely the time wasted waiting for the other person to arrive. To Rae, being on time was a sign of respect, an acknowledgment that everyone had urgent things to do and important places to be. They didn't think it was something they could overlook in someone they were interested in. But they also didn't know whether Julie's tardiness was an actual problem or a series of unfortunate coincidences.

Out of the corner of their eye, a spot of yellow glided across the green grass, and Rae did a double take. They almost didn't recognize Julie.

Her hair wasn't in its usual ponytail, but rather, it rippled around her shoulders like a shimmering black waterfall. Gone were the scrubs or form-fitting workout gear, and in their place was a pale-yellow sundress that showed off Julie's shoulders, cut low enough to reveal a hint of cleavage. It followed the taper of her torso to her narrow waist before blossoming outward in a flowing knee-length skirt.

She was beautiful, stunning, gorgeous. And Rae was struck with the sudden desire to strip off that simple, summery dress to explore all the treasures hidden underneath.

She stopped to say hello to a teammate and the smile she gave them made Rae inexplicably delighted and jealous at the same time. Their whole body had come alive at the sight of Julie, but a hint of envy grated across their skin when Julie didn't immediately come over to greet them.

"Oh yeah, they definitely have a crush," Fran said cheekily.

Rae dragged their eyes away from Julie to glare at

their two friends, but Fran and Beile grinned back at them, annoyingly pleased with themselves.

"Maybe it's a good thing I went mountain biking, eh?" Fran spoke to Beile, though her words were obviously meant for Rae. "If I hadn't broken my arm, we never would've had this delightful development."

"Shut up." Rae tried to sound grumpy, but the words came out a little too bashful for their liking. They focused on turning the hotdogs and sausages over on the grill.

Beile gasped dramatically. "Oh look! She's talking to your grandmother."

Rae's head snapped up, gaze immediately zeroing in on the park bench where they'd left PoPo earlier. Sure enough, Julie was pulling over a lawn chair to sit next to PoPo's wheelchair.

Rae's breath caught as they were seized by a spike of panic. They hadn't anticipated PoPo meeting Julie today. In hindsight, it was obvious they would cross paths, but for some reason, the possibility had never occurred to Rae.

It didn't necessarily mean anything, Rae told themself. They had never told PoPo Julie's name. There were plenty of unfamiliar faces at the picnic. What were the chances PoPo would put two and two together?

Pretty high, if Rae was honest with themself. They needed to intervene before PoPo said something inappropriate.

"Here." They shoved the barbecue tongs into Beile's hands. "Watch this for me."

Without waiting for a response, they took the plate of cooked hamburger patties from Fran and headed toward the picnic table.

Both PoPo and Julie looked up as they approached. Julie smiled shyly at them, a beautiful pink dusting the tops of her cheeks, and a warm, fuzzy feeling spread across Rae's chest at the sight. PoPo, on the other hand, grinned like a scheming villain—she knew *exactly* who Julie was.

"You made it." They tried to stay cool and nonchalant, like Julie was no one special, just another paddler on the team.

"Yeah." She winced lightly. "Sorry, I'm late."

"Did you know Julie's a doctor?" PoPo said, putting so much emphasis on that last word, it was almost comical.

"Yes, PoPo, I did."

"She works at St. Mitchell's Hospital."

"Yes, I know."

"And she delivers babies!" PoPo's entire face lit up like it was some miraculous revelation.

"Yes, I know that too."

With each exchange, Julie's blush grew and grew until there were two bright pink spots on her cheeks. Her smile held a hint of embarrassment, but there was also pride and gratification. She snuck a glance toward Rae, almost as if she wasn't sure how Rae would react to their grandmother's praise of her.

Guilt slid through Rae like a slippery serpent. It wasn't that they weren't impressed with Julie's professional success—they were. But it often butted up against the demands of dragon boat, and Rae couldn't help but be protective of their baby. Not everyone was as dedicated to dragon boat as Rae was, and that was fine. But then they shouldn't commit to the demanding schedule. And if they hadn't needed to fill Fran's seat so badly, Rae wasn't sure they'd be as willing to let Julie's lateness slide.

"Are you going to eat all of that?"

PoPo's question interrupted Rae's musings, and it took them a moment to figure out what she was talking about. PoPo gestured to the plate they still held. Only then did they remember they were holding a pile of burger patties that were quickly growing cold.

"I should go put this down." Rae inched backward, not sure if leaving Julie with PoPo was such a good idea.

"And make a plate for Julie too!"

"Oh, you don't have to do that. I can make one myself." Julie made to stand, but PoPo gently grabbed her arm and pulled her back down.

"No, Rae can do it. Go. Go!" PoPo made a shooing motion with her hand, leaving Rae with no choice.

They shot Julie an apologetic look before hurrying away. The faster they moved, the sooner they would be back to do damage control. At the picnic table, they slapped together a hamburger with lettuce, tomatoes, and sriracha mayo, and filled the rest of the plate with crushed cucumber salad. Then with a fork, a bottle of water, and a couple napkins, they hightailed it back to Julie and PoPo.

Julie was laughing at something. Her head was

thrown back, highlighting the long column of her neck, the smooth expanse of her chest, and the delicate swell of her breasts. Her hair slid over her bare shoulders, so glossy Rae could've sworn they heard the hissing glide of silk against skin.

"You laugh, but it's true. Every single word!"

"What's true?" Rae asked as they handed the plate to Julie and sat down on the grass in front of them.

PoPo ignored them completely. "Rae was a giant baby. Over nine pounds!"

Julie chuckled, glancing at Rae like she was trying to picture Rae as an oversized infant. "That's a big baby."

"Took their mother days to get them out. Poor girl."

Rae had heard this story countless times before, and every time, it got wilder and more dramatic. One time, PoPo claimed that Rae's mother had been in labor for a week. Another time, fetus Rae had been breached. Rae had no idea what the real story was anymore.

Julie's eyebrows shot up in concern. "Days? The doctor didn't do a cesarean?"

PoPo shrugged. "Maybe. I don't remember. All I know is Rae was so big, I could barely hold them up."

Rae rolled their eyes, then met Julie's gaze. They shared a look filled with amusement and understanding, and that warm, fuzzy feeling in Rae's chest grew.

In that moment, Rae couldn't remember why they were so wary about getting involved with Julie. She was smart and beautiful, and she had a gentleness that was lined with incredible strength. Rae couldn't help but be drawn toward her.

No one was perfect, after all. God knew Rae had plenty of failings of their own. Every relationship required some sort of compromise, right? Maybe they were being too rigid, too harsh. Maybe they should give Julie a chance.

SEVEN

JULIE

STANDING across the street from The Flower Shoppe, Julie hesitated. The sign above the store was the same dark forest green as Rae's shirt from that day at the hospital, with the name of the store in blush pink old-timey font. Through the window was a jungle of plants in varying shades of green.

The door opened and for a moment, Julie stood frozen with fear that Rae would step out and see her there. But it was just a customer cradling a paper-wrapped bouquet in his arms as he headed down the street.

This was ridiculous. If she wanted to go in and say hello, she should just go in. There was no point in loitering out on the street like some creep. The thing was, she didn't know whether her presence would be welcome.

The team picnic over the weekend was lovely. She hadn't been to any social gatherings outside the hospital's staff lounge in ages and she'd forgotten how much fun parties could be. She hadn't expected to meet Rae's grandmother either, but once she'd sat down next to the elderly woman, she hadn't wanted to be anywhere else.

Julie hadn't known any of her own grandparents. They'd all passed by the time she was born. She also never had extended family around while growing up and her parents never told her much about their family back in Hong Kong.

She was a bit embarrassed to admit how fascinating it was to watch Rae's PoPo talk about them and their family so much. It made her wonder about her own family's stories and how little she knew of them.

And while PoPo recounted one tale after another, Rae lounged on the grass by Julie's feet. The fabric of their fitted shorts stretched around thick thighs, and the body-hugging black tank top offset the bright tattoos on their arms. They kept shooting smoldering looks in Julie's direction, lips quirking up into sexy smiles whenever PoPo's exaggerations got out of hand. By the time the party ended, Julie had felt overheated and it had nothing to do with the sun.

It was a few days later and Julie couldn't get the image of Rae out of her head. So here she was, standing outside their store, wanting to go inside, but terrified of what she might find.

Rae might not even be there, for goodness's sake. They could be out on a delivery or running errands. They wouldn't even have to know that Julie stopped by. She could go in and pretend she was a regular customer, and if Rae wasn't there, she'd just buy some flowers and leave.

Contingency plans drawn up in her mind, Julie took a steadying breath, looked both ways, then crossed the street.

A little bell jingled when she pulled open the door, and once she stepped inside, she stopped short. It was like she'd walked through a portal into another world. The temperature was several degrees cooler and the air smelled mossy and organic. Plants of all shapes and sizes filled the shelves lining the walls. Giant trees sat in pots on the floor. Baskets with trailing vines hung from the ceiling. In the midst of all the green were bursts of red, orange, yellow, purple. The sound of trickling water played like a soundtrack in the background.

Julie followed the narrow winding path from the door, her fingers brushing against the cool leaves, the scent of earth and grass tickling her nose. Goosebumps sprouted along her arms from the chill in the air.

"Hi! Welcome to The Flower Shoppe!" A younger woman called out cheerfully from behind the service counter. "Can I help you with anything?"

For a moment, Julie forgot where she was and why she was there.

Then from somewhere at the back of the store came a loud gasp of pain and "Fuck!"

The woman behind the counter spun around. "Rae? You okay?"

Julie didn't think, she just moved. Rounding the end of the counter, she slipped between an opening between a large shelving unit and the flower fridge. The space at the back of the store wasn't big and every available surface was occupied with carefully labeled boxes.

Rae stood at a banged-up table covered with bundles of flowers, pressing a paper towel into one hand. Red was already seeping through.

Julie immediately slipped into doctor mode, pushing aside all the nerves she'd been feeling before. Rae went from the object of her constant thoughts to a patient who needed emergency medical care.

"Did you cut yourself?" She took Rae's injured hand and carefully lifted the paper towel away. She grimaced when she saw it was already sopping wet from use and dotted with smudges of black and green. Blood oozed from the cut, enough to obscure just how deep it went.

"Julie?" Rae's surprise was obvious, but they didn't object as Julie examined the wound. "What are you doing here?"

Julie ignored the question and instead dragged them over to the sink. "Where's your first aid kit?" She turned on the cold water and stuck Rae's hand underneath.

Rae hissed but didn't pull their hand away. "In the bathroom. Raufikat?"

"Yup!" The woman from the front darted into a small room off to the side that Julie hadn't noticed.

"You really shouldn't use a dirty paper towel," Julie scolded under her breath, bending over Rae's hand as the blood washed away. "It isn't sterile. You could get an infection"

"I just grabbed whatever was available," Rae

defended themself with a hint of amusement in their voice. "It wasn't like I had time to go digging for sterilized gauze."

"Here you go." Raufikat came back and popped open the small first aid kit.

Julie breathed a sigh of relief that it was fully stocked, if a little old. The packaging on the gauze was starting to turn a little yellow, but the bottle of antibiotic gel hadn't yet expired. Julie grabbed the gauze, ripped the package open, and used the gauze to apply pressure to the cut.

"It isn't too deep," Julie said, holding Rae's hand in both of her own. "You shouldn't need stitches."

"I know. This isn't the first time I've cut myself with a knife. But thank you. I could get used to this kind of treatment." Rae's voice was rumbly and low, and only then did Julie realize how close they were standing. The gentle vibrations of their voice seemed to travel through their clasped hands and reverberate all the way down to Julie's toes. Along the way, heat pooled between her legs.

Julie glanced up and their gaze collided with Rae's, the impact stealing her breath away. Standing this close, Julie could see all the variations of brown in their irises. Their brows were elegantly shaped but strong, and their nose was just a little bit crooked.

When they exhaled, their breath tickled Julie's cheek, making her lips part with a silent gasp. Rae's gaze dropped to her mouth and her tongue slipped out to wet her suddenly dry lips.

Desire curled through Julie, sensitizing her nipples and electrifying her skin. She squeezed her thighs together as she grew wet, and a shiver of arousal shot up her spine.

Rae brought their free hand to Julie's arm, running it from her shoulder to her elbow and up again. "Cold?"

Julie swayed closer to Rae and shook her head. No, she wasn't cold. If anything, she was warm and growing hotter.

Rae's hand drifted up to Julie's jaw. Their fingers slipped into the hair falling out of Julie's ponytail. Their thumb caressed her cheek, and her eyes fluttered closed. Her pulse accelerated into a steady thrum, coursing through her and making her ache.

"Julie." Rae sounded almost tortured, like they were trying to fight this attraction between them and losing. "I want to kiss you."

Her pussy clenched at the simple statement of fact. Rae, so edgy and cool, wanted to kiss her, and suddenly that was the only thing Julie wanted too.

"Please," she breathed.

Rae didn't waste another second.

They fitted their lips against Julie's, pillowy soft, though slightly chapped. When they moved, pressing and brushing, with just a tiny bit of tongue, a desperate hunger roared to life in her.

She plastered herself against Rae, arms going around Rae's back to hold them together. Rae's body was the perfect combination of hard and soft. Their muscles shifted under Julie's palms, and their subtle curves fit against Julie's like they were two interconnecting puzzle pieces.

Rae's hand on her cheek slid all the way into her hair, dislodging her hair tie until it fell out. They angled her just the way they wanted her and when they ran their tongue across Julie's lips, Julie met it with her own. Rae let out a low growl and hauled Julie against them.

Julie's entire body was on fire and she trembled with barely contained need. It had been a long time since she'd been kissed, and even longer since she'd been kissed like this. Like her lover was starved and the only source of sustenance was Julie herself. She wanted to be consumed and devoured. She wanted to be reduced to nothing but a mass of quivering flesh.

A tiny bell jingled, and the high-pitched sound tore through the veil of arousal that had descended upon them. They jumped apart, eyes wide with lust and lips bruised from their kiss. Julie's hair was a tangled mess around her shoulders and her panties were almost soaked right through. She could think of nothing else but climbing onto Rae and grinding them together until they'd both come their brains out.

But voices from the front of the store echoed back to them, reminding Julie they were technically still in public and she had interrupted Rae at work.

"Sorry." The word tumbled from her lips. This was most certainly not what she'd had in mind when she crossed the street to enter the store. "I didn't mean to..."

Rae's eyes narrowed dangerously, but instead of the prickle of intimidation Julie was used to, she felt another rush of desire flood her system. "Don't be sorry. I'm not."

A shudder ran through Julie at the gruffness in Rae's voice.

"Store closes at six. I can be out of here by six-twenty." The implication was clear.

Julie gulped as her body hummed in anticipation. She nodded, the movement somewhat jerky. And in a voice that sounded too husky to be her own, she said, "I'll text you my address."

EIGHT

RAE

RAE HAD NEVER CLOSED up the shop so quickly in all the years they owned the store. Raufikat had offered to do it herself—eyes gleaming with amusement—so Rae could get out early, and they were a little ashamed they had considered taking her up on it. But in the end, Rae couldn't let themself succumb to their desires so easily.

It was nearly seven by the time Rae arrived at the address Julie had sent them. It was a condo in the West Don Lands, right down by the lake. The building lobby had double height ceilings with fancy, modern decor. And after Julie buzzed them in, they took the elevator right up to the penthouse.

Rae clutched the bouquet of flowers they'd brought with them, suddenly seized by a bout of nerves. It wasn't the typical jitters that came at the beginning of any rela-tionship. This thing with Julie felt more significant. Like the outcome would either be magnificent or a fiasco and nothing in between. The consequences could change Rae's life—they just weren't sure in which direction.

They knocked and a split second later, the door opened.

Julie was freshly showered, cheeks a little pink and hair still slightly damp. She was wearing leggings that hugged her shapely legs and an oversized t-shirt that hung off one shoulder. Rae stared at that shoulder for a few long moments, memorizing the delicate curve, before dragging their gaze back to Julie's face. The smile gracing her lips looked just as apprehensive and anticipatory as Rae felt.

"Please come in." She stepped to the side and held the door open for Rae.

"These are for you." Rae held out the lilacs they'd carefully wrapped in cellophane. The purple flowers reminded them of Julie. Incredibly fragrant, lilacs had delicate flowers and yet, the plant itself was surprisingly hearty. As bashful and soft as Julie often seemed, she was also as strong and tough as they came.

"Oh, wow, thank you." Julie took the flowers and brought them to her nose. Her eyes drifted shut as she took a deep breath, her smile growing with delight.

She was mesmerizing, and Rae felt themself fall for Julie a little bit, right then and there.

"How's your hand?" Julie asked as she led the way into the kitchen.

It hurt like a bitch, hot and throbbing under the bandage Julie had put on it. Rae had been processing the new shipment of flowers all afternoon, dunking their hands into cold water again and again. Their hands had been mostly numb when they sliced their palm along the outer edge under the pinky, but now that they'd thawed, the area around the wound felt like it was on fire.

"It's fine," Rae said, tearing open the cellophane around the flowers while Julie filled a vase. "Do you have sharp scissors?"

Julie handed them a pair of kitchen shears. "How come you were using a knife at the shop?"

Rae cut the ends off each stem and arranged the flowers in the vase to make a perfect centerpiece. "Faster than using scissors. And easier to sharpen when they get dull."

"Also easier to cut yourself on." Julie leaned her hip on the counter, arms folded across her chest, pushing her breasts up invitingly. She watched Rae with an expression that was half scolding and half teasing.

"Good thing I know a doctor who can patch me up," Rae teased right back. They made a few last tweaks to the flowers in the vase, then picked it up and held it out for Julie.

As Julie moved to take it, her hands settled over Rae's, and even though they could tell that Julie had a firm grip on the vase, they didn't let their hands fall away. They stood there, staring into each other's eyes, both holding the vase between them. A beat passed in silence, and Rae's heart thumped faster and stronger with each second.

Julie's lips parted. Her breasts rose and fell with each breath. The memory of their kiss earlier curled through

Rae and settled low in their stomach. They wanted this woman. And she wanted them back.

Neither of them spoke as, together, they set the vase back on the counter. Then Rae took Julie by the waist and tugged her in until the softness of her breasts pressed against their chest. Julie's quiet gasp echoed in their ear, and the shudder that ran through her made Rae shudder too.

They ran their nose across her cheek to her ear, then down her neck. Julie dropped her head back, giving Rae better access, and Rae took in a deep, lungful of air. She smelled sweet, like vanilla and honey, and Rae wanted to lick every inch of her body, taste every inch of her skin.

Heat pooled in their groin, and their stomach tightened with arousal. They slid their hands down to Julie's ass, filling their palms, and squeezed. Julie let out a soft whimper and rose up on her toes. She lifted one leg to wrap around Rae's hip, tilting her pelvis up to grind her mound against Rae's.

Rae buried their face into the crook of Julie's neck, her hair falling over Rae's forehead. Goddamn, she felt good in their arms. Soft and pliant and trembling with barely restrained desire. Rae wanted to see her explode with pleasure and fall apart with release. They wanted to be the one who made it happen.

"Bedroom," they growled.

Julie blinked as if she was trying to clear the lust from her mind, then she grabbed Rae's hand and dragged them through the living room toward the other end of the apartment.

The second they stepped inside the bedroom, Rae stopped short and yanked Julie backward, her back against their front. Rae slid one hand under Julie's shirt, gliding it over her soft stomach to cup a full, tender breast. The other hand slipped under the waistband of her leggings and down in between her legs.

Rae growled at what they found. Julie wasn't wearing a bra or any underwear. Her nipple pebbled against their palm. Their fingers glided easily through her wetness to find her swollen clit.

"Oh god," Julie cried, turning her head toward Rae.

They captured her lips in a sloppy, messy kiss, and Julie clung to them as they worked her over. Breasts squeezed. Nipples pinched. Clit rubbed and flicked until Julie's breathing grew erratic and her whole body went taut with an orgasm, and still, Rae maintained the stimulation, unrelenting, building Julie up to a second orgasm in as many minutes.

Julie went lax in their arms, limbs heavy as aftershocks rolled through her. Rae carefully maneuvered her onto the bed where she lay sprawled out, hair in a dark halo around her head.

She gazed up at them with heavy-lidded eyes. Holding her gaze, Rae lifted their wet hand and licked Julie's desire off their fingers. Musky and just a bit tangy, the flavor exploded on Rae's tongue, making their mouth water for more. A shudder ran through Julie as she watched.

Under Julie's unwavering scrutiny, Rae stripped, tossing their clothes over a chair in the corner of the room. Then they approached the bed and rid Julie of her clothes too. Rae took a moment to appreciate the view.

Dark areolas topped perfectly round breasts. The creamy, pale skin of her stomach dimpled at her belly button. Her bush was trimmed short, and as Rae admired her shapely legs, Julie slowly spread them wide.

Rae set one knee in between them, then slowly lowered themself on top of Julie. She welcomed their weight, hooking one leg around their hip and arching up to rub herself against their front. Julie ran a hand across the back of their head, and the sensation of her palm over the bristles sent heat shooting straight through Rae's body.

Julie lifted her knee, planting her foot on the bed and pressing her thigh right against the juncture of Rae's legs. They ground down against Julie as their lips tangled in a dance that made them leak all over Julie's hip.

They trailed kisses down Julie's neck, across her collarbone, and down to her chest. With one breast cradled in their hand, they laved at the nipple with their tongue. Flicking then sucking, grazing the sensitive flesh with their teeth. They took as much as they could fit into their mouth, kneading it between their lips.

"Oh god, Rae!" Julie held them to her with both hands on the back of their head, her whole body vibrating under Rae's touch.

They ground down against Julie, already primed from making Julie come twice in a row. And with Julie's breast in their mouth, they came, pleasure rocketing through them so hard they saw stars.

Julie let out a cry, lifting off the bed as yet another orgasm claimed her. It added fuel to Rae's pleasure, making it crest again before they collapsed, drained, on top of Julie.

Languidly, they rolled to the side, bringing Julie with them. They curled around each other, legs all knotted together, arms looped around backs.

"Wow," Julie breathed, chest still heaving with exertion.

Rae couldn't help the smile that tugged on their lips. Gratification that went far beyond physical settled warm and weighty inside them. Watching Julie come was way more satisfying than they could've imagined. And knowing they were the one who brought Julie there made it all that more so.

They wanted to do it again. All night long. For days on end. They had gotten a small taste of Julie, and they feared it would never be enough.

NINE

JULIE

"THIS IS the nicest and saddest kitchen I've ever seen." Rae stood in front of the fridge, hands on hips, staring into its empty insides.

"Um... thank you?" Julie responded from where she sat at the kitchen island. She was still feeling loose and a little buzzy from all the orgasms Rae had wrung out of her. She'd suggested they stay in bed and just order delivery, but Rae had wanted to poke around her kitchen instead.

Rae glanced over their shoulder at her, a slight wince around their eyes. "That wasn't really a compliment."

"I know," Julie said, contrite. "But I'm at work so often, it doesn't make sense to keep the fridge fully stocked. Besides, I'm not much of a cook."

Rae sighed and closed the fridge, turning instead to the pantry to examine its meager offerings. "So what? You just order out all the time?" They reached in and started pulling out things Julie hadn't even known were in there.

"Or the hospital cafeteria."

Rae set down an open package of dry spaghetti and a can of tomato sauce. From the freezer, they somehow materialized bags of frozen vegetables that Julie suspected were horribly frostbitten. "Your sodium levels must be through the roof."

Julie shrugged. She didn't remember the last time she'd gotten a physical. She wasn't even sure she'd ever had her sodium levels tested. "I try to eat healthy. Salads and stuff."

From the unimpressed look Rae shot her, it was clear they didn't believe her. "When's the last time you had a home-cooked meal?"

She gave it some thought before answering. "The team picnic?"

The scowl Rae pinned her with would've been scary if Julie hadn't known they were just looking out for her well-being. It had been a very, very long time since she'd had anyone do that, and she squirmed a little, not sure how she should feel about it.

She'd worked hard to get to where she was today, learning how to be self-sufficient and relying only on herself. The thought of letting go, of letting someone else in, was just a tiny bit scary. But it also sounded nice. Like relief. Like reprieve.

"That doesn't count," Rae said, opening and closing cabinets and drawers like this was their kitchen instead of

Julie's. "I meant actually home-cooked, like from scratch. Not stuff from the frozen food aisle."

Julie gave them a sheepish smile. "Doctors are kind of notorious for being unhealthy. I'm actually not that bad, comparatively."

Rae shook their head in resignation as they set a pot of water to boil on the stove. "You need someone to look after you."

"Are you volunteering?" Julie snapped her mouth shut the second she heard herself speak, and her cheeks immediately began to heat. She had no idea where that question had come from and no idea what kind of answer she was hoping for.

Rae stilled, a bag of frozen vegetables in hand, and slowly turned to look at her. The expression in their eyes was dark and dangerous, and Julie's pussy clenched as desire pooled between her legs. Her survival instinct told her to run. Her libido had her glued to the spot, ensnared by Rae's calculating scrutiny.

"Are you offering me the job?"

Julie gulped at the roughness in Rae's voice. They set down the bag of veggies and stalked around the island toward her. Turning her to face them, they pushed her knees apart to slot themself in between. Staring up at them, Julie's lips parted as she struggled to catch her breath.

She didn't dare move when Rae lifted a hand and oh-so-gently threaded their fingers through her hair. The light tug had Julie's eyes fluttering shut. Fingers ghosted over her cheek, her jaw, under her chin.

Rae's breath puffed against her skin right before their lips made contact with Julie's. It was a soft kiss, nothing more than a press of lips against lips, but Julie felt it right down to the soles of her feet. It didn't last long, but even those few seconds left them both panting, foreheads resting together as they caught their breaths.

Rae's question echoed in Julie's ears. Was she looking for someone to take care of her? Did she want Rae to be that person? Julie had a sneaking suspicion that her answer to both questions was a resounding yes.

But they just met. They hardly knew anything about each other. Julie's work schedule was demanding, and she didn't know what she could commit to after this dragon boat season was over. Was this really something she wanted to pursue when it would mean rearranging her entire life?

Rae didn't press her for an answer but rather threw her a rakish grin before returning to the stove. They added salt and olive oil to the water before dumping in the dry spaghetti. The vegetables had frozen into one large mass, which they stuck into the microwave to defrost.

Julie watched in silence as Rae cooked, feeling like she was standing on the precipice of something big. If she stepped forward, would she be met with solid ground or empty air? The easy option would be to back away and stay in the safety of what was known and comfortable. But is that what she really wanted? Is that where she wanted to live out the rest of her life?

In almost no time at all, Rae was plating up two

dishes of spaghetti and topping them off with grated parmesan cheese that somehow hadn't yet gone off in the fridge. Julie slipped from her seat at the island and collected cutlery to set the dining table. When they sat down opposite each other, she took in the thrown-together meal in awe. She would never have been able to pull together anything so appetizing with the time and ingredients she'd had on hand.

"Oh my god," she mumbled around a mouthful of pasta.

"Is it okay?" Rae had the temerity to look uncertain as if this wasn't one of the best things Julie had tasted in a long time.

"Are you kidding me? This is amazing!" Her stomach gurgled in approval as she twirled her fork in the spaghetti. She hadn't realized how hungry she was until she'd taken the first bite.

Rae shook their head with a furtive smile on their lips.

"What?" Julie asked, laughing, her cheeks feeling warm under Rae's scrutiny. "Why are you looking at me like that? This is really good!"

Rae tilted their head and furrowed their brow skeptically. "It's decent, but nothing spectacular. We need to work on raising your standards."

Julie ducked her head and gave Rae a small smile with a tinge of embarrassment. "I'd like that," she said softly, and she knew it was true. She liked this light, bubbly feeling Rae managed to bring out in her. She also liked the edgy and slightly menacing vibe Rae gave off sometimes. Even the things she didn't like about Rae—when they were abrasive and short and downright rude—were tempered by their kindness, humility, and generosity.

Taking that step forward was without a doubt one of the scariest things Julie had faced in her life. But she wanted to know what was beyond that ledge. She didn't want to look back on this moment and regret not being brave enough to find out.

She reached her hand across the table and Rae slotted theirs inside. "Stay tonight?" she asked in barely a whisper.

Rae smiled, slow and sweet. Their eyes shone with something that made Julie all warm inside. They took Julie's hand and brought it up to their lips for a kiss against the palm. "Sure."

Later, after they'd finished eating and had cleaned up the kitchen, they retired back to the bedroom. Julie laid back on the bed as Rae lavished her with kisses, licks, and love bites. They worked their way down Julie's body, pushing her knees apart to fit their wide shoulders in between.

Julie watched, trembling, as Rae lowered their head and planted a kiss right on top of her mound. Open-mouthed. Tongue slipping out and finding the folds of her labia. Sliding in between until it made contact with Julie's already swollen clit.

She gasped at the touch and cried out as Rae played with it, rubbing, twirling, sucking, making Julie wet with their saliva and her own juices. Then Rae brought their hand to the entrance of Julie's body and slowly inserted one finger.

Julie couldn't help clenching around the invasion. It had been so long since anything besides herself and her toys had been inside her. Since she'd been at the mercy of someone else's hands.

Rae's mouth continued working over her clit while they fucked her with that single digit. Thrusting. Twisting. Curling. Hitting all the sensitive spots inside Julie that she'd almost forgotten about.

"More, please Rae. I need more," she begged, clutching the sheets beneath her in desperation.

She felt Rae smile against her a moment before a second finger joined the first. Rae didn't give her much time to adjust to the added girth before adding yet another. She was stretched so wide. Rae's knuckles were jammed hard against the outside. And they wiggled their fingers back and forth inside her, pressing up against the front wall of her pussy.

"Oh my god!" Julie arched up into Rae's mouth as pleasure burst through her, exploding from the duel assault between her legs to the other extremities of her body. Wave after wave, unrelenting, as Rae continued their ministrations. Julie couldn't tell whether it was a series of orgasms in quick succession, or if it was one long orgasm drawn out over minutes.

By the time her vision cleared and she could think again, Rae was lapping at her vagina, licking up all the wetness she had gushed. There was a wet spot on the bed underneath her.

She tugged on Rae's shoulder, urging them up so she could kiss them. The bottom half of their face was covered in Julie's desire, and when Julie got her mouth on theirs, she could taste herself on their tongue.

She drew her hands down Rae's body, flattening her palms against their chest until their nipples hardened into points. Then down their flat, washboard stomach, and finally to that sacred spot between their legs. They were just as wet down there as their face was, and Julie's fingers were soaked in no time.

"Inside?" she asked in a hoarse whisper against Rae's lips.

They nodded, and Julie easily slid two fingers right in.

Rae hissed, reaching down to grab Julie's wrist. But instead of stopping her or pulling her hand away, they pressed her hand deeper and held it there. Then they fucked her hand.

"Yes, right there," Rae murmured when Julie curled her fingers and angled her hand so the heel jutted against Rae's clit. "Just like that. It's perfect."

Rae buried their face into the crook of Julie's neck while they used Julie's hand to get off. It was the hottest thing Julie had ever seen. This strong, confident, sexy person taking their pleasure from Julie. Entirely unapologetic. They knew what they wanted, what they needed, and they didn't hesitate to demand it, to claim it.

The grip on her wrist was almost painful as Rae held her exactly where they wanted her. She felt teeth sink into the juncture between her neck and shoulder. Rae rocked above her, every muscle taut and primed to explode.

When they came, it was like a vise clamping down on Julie's hand. Rae's inner muscles constricted and twitched around her fingers. Their body tensed and shook, and Julie held them close to her until they eventually calmed.

Julie closed her eyes to savor the moment. Both of them sweaty and wet. Skin sticking to skin, and the smell of their sex hanging in the air. The weight of Rae's body on hers was solid and grounding.

Yes, this was scary. But every good thing came with some amount of fear, didn't it? Julie wasn't about to let that stand in the way of her happiness.

TEN

RAE

RAE WAS awake before the sun rose, lips already curled in a smile. They never slept well in unfamiliar beds, especially the first night. But this time, they didn't really mind.

Julie was curled up against them, bottom lip pushed out in an adorable pout, arm and leg slung over Rae's body like she was afraid they would disappear in the middle of the night. Her hair was a cloud of black against the white pillowcase. Her bare shoulder, collarbone, and neck looked good enough to devour, and Rae's groin clenched with a spike of desire.

They hadn't come over intending to stay the night. But when Julie asked them in that small, tentative voice, there was no way Rae was leaving. Seeing Julie's kitchen had ignited a protectiveness in Rae they hadn't felt with anyone other than maybe PoPo. But even then, it wasn't quite the same.

It was no surprise to Rae that Julie's apartment was

impressive. On the top floor of the mid-rise condo, it was strategically placed to capture panoramic views of Lake Ontario. The floors were a pale hardwood. The decor was modern and sleek. The kitchen was fully equipped with every high-end appliance Rae could imagine—and almost nothing edible.

Julie wasn't kidding when she said her career dominated her life. This was an apartment of someone who had enough money to buy it, but not enough time to live in it. That was no way to live, and Rae felt this deep-seated desire to help Julie fix it.

Were they being foolish in getting this attached to Julie? For all the protectiveness Julie ignited in them and all the unsubtle hints PoPo kept dropping, they had very different priorities for themself. There was no guarantee Julie would want to change, and Rae didn't like the idea of always being passed over for Julie's career. Perhaps they were just asking for their heart to be broken when their differences finally came to a head.

Julie stirred, snuggling in closer to Rae and letting out a contented sigh. "You're still here," she murmured, voice groggy with sleep.

Rae glanced at Julie, but her eyes were still closed. "I said I would stay. Did you think I would sneak out?"

She lifted a shoulder in a lazy shrug. "I dunno. I thought maybe it was a dream."

Rae's heart ached at the comment, leaving them at a loss for how to respond. What did it say about Julie that she didn't think Rae was real? That her expectations were so low that Rae keeping their word was considered fantastical?

Rae gathered her into their arms and pressed a kiss to their forehead. "Not a dream," they whispered in the small space between them.

Julie hugged them back, pressing herself even closer.

Who were they kidding? Yes, maybe this was a foolish endeavor. Maybe they would end up with a broken heart. But they were already in far deeper than they realized. They couldn't pull back now. They couldn't step away. Whether they liked it or not, they had to see this through.

They both eventually climbed out of bed, and Rae ventured into the kitchen in search of caffeine. They laughed when they found Julie's stash. Of all the things she could stock in her kitchen, of course it would be dozens of gourmet coffee beans, all vacuum-sealed and stored in the dark next to the high-end espresso machine. The thing had so many knobs and buttons Rae didn't even know where to start. They stared at it for several long minutes, afraid they would break the damn thing.

They waited for Julie to emerge from the bathroom, already dressed for the dragon boat practice they were both due at shortly.

"I, uh, couldn't figure this out," Rae said, waving their hand at the espresso machine.

"Oh, here. Let me show you." Julie pulled out a mini-scale and a single-serving coffee bean grinder. She moved like a barista, pressing the grounds into that thingy with the handle, and snapping the entire contraption into the machine itself. She hit a couple buttons and the machine rumbled to life.

Leaning back against the counter, Rae watched in amazement, their jaw practically resting on their chest, and Julie blushed when she caught sight of them.

"I was a barista in high school and undergrad," she explained. "Can't cook for my life, but I can make every kind of coffee-related concoction under the sun."

She held out the miniature espresso cup, and Rae took it, bringing it to their lips. The dark brew was bitter but rich, a complex combination of flavors that exploded on their tongue. A bit fruity, a bit chocolatey, the drink was creamy as it slid down their throat.

"Wow, this is... wow." They blinked at the cup, already wanting another even though they hadn't yet finished the first. This was an entirely new side of Julie they never would have guessed existed.

Julie rolled her eyes as a smile graced her lips. "You don't have to look so impossibly shocked. I'm not *completely* useless in the kitchen."

"No! That's not—!" Properly chastised, Rae pulled Julie between their outstretched legs and wrapped an arm around her waist. They lifted the cup between them. "This is genuinely impressive. I'm not just saying that."

The blush on Julie's cheeks darkened. "I always figured if this whole doctor thing didn't work out, I might try opening a coffee shop or something."

Rae perked up at the idea. "Really?"

"Yeah, I don't know. I haven't given it much thought," Julie said, shrugging and ducking her head.

Rae placed a finger under her chin and lifted it until Julie met their gaze. "I think it's a great idea." And suddenly, they had this image of Julie quitting her medical career to open a coffee shop next to the flower store. They could knock down the wall in between to turn it into one big space—coffee, tea, and pastries; tables and chairs for customers to hang out; plants and flowers everywhere, creating a green oasis in the middle of the city.

It was selfish of them, they knew. Julie was a successful doctor. It was an important job, and she clearly loved it. She shouldn't give it up just because Rae wasn't fond of the schedule it demanded.

Julie's smile turned whimsical. "Maybe one day."

The imaginary joint flower and coffee shop wouldn't leave Rae alone the entire ride from Julie's house to the rowing club, even during the detour they took to Rae's place so they could pick up their training gear. By the time they arrived—early—Rae was already mentally arranging the layout of the space.

Beile pulled up to the clubhouse not long after they did, and she stopped short the moment she laid eyes on them. She spun around, surveying the parking lot, then spun back to them.

"What?" Rae demanded, regretting the question the moment it left their lips. It sounded way too defensive, and from the way Beile's eyes narrowed in scrutiny, she definitely picked up on it.

She pointed at both of them. "Did you two... you did, didn't you?"

Julie's cheeks went tomato red, defeating any hope Rae had of denial.

Beile gasped, both hands flying to her mouth. "Ohmygod, you did!" She bounced on her feet like she couldn't physically contain her excitement.

"Whoa, let's dial it back a bit." Rae gestured with their hands to keep Beile calm, even though a part of them thrilled at the reaction they were getting. It was affirming to have a friend be so enthusiastic and supportive, but there were still too many unknowns between them to start announcing things to everyone.

"I *knew* it! I knew you guys would be perfect for each other!"

Julie's blush spread to her ears and down her neck, and Rae's protectiveness reared its head.

"Can you just chill?" Rae looped their arm around Beile's shoulders and dragged her away from the open area just as more of their teammates started pulling into the parking lot. "It's still new, and we're not ready to broadcast it to the whole world yet."

"Oh, come on!" Beile whined. "You're lesbians. You should be booking a U-Haul by now."

Rae had always hated that stereotype, though the idea didn't feel as irritating with Julie as it should have. They didn't want to think too much about what that meant. "No— we're not— Beile." Rae infused as much warning into their voice as they could. "Please."

"Okay, okay!" Beile held up both hands in surrender. "I'll keep my mouth shut... for now." She shot Rae one more mischievous look, then slipped out from under their arm.

With a sigh, Rae turned to Julie with an apology ready on their lips. But instead of the blushing and bashful Julie they expected to find, Julie's head was bowed as she glared at her phone.

Rae braced themself, already knowing what was coming. "What's wrong?"

Julie lifted her gaze to them, guilt written plain across her face. "It's the hospital."

Rae's stomach sank, and every single doubt they'd ever had about this relationship came rushing up to the surface.

"It's one of my high-risk patients," Julie said, taking a few steps closer, but stopping just short of Rae. "She needs an emergency cesarean."

Can't another doctor do it? The question raced through Rae's mind, but they didn't let themself indulge it.

Yes, perhaps there was another doctor who could perform the surgery. And yes, Julie definitely needed a better work-life balance. But this was what made her so good at her job—she cared deeply about her patients, and they trusted her with their lives. Who was Rae to demand she stay? What right did they have to judge her for her priorities?

They nodded, and their voice was tight when they spoke. "You should go."

Julie hesitated. "Are you sure?"

For a split second, Rae thought maybe she would

choose them over her job, but it was fleeting. This was who Julie was; she had never pretended to be anything else. Rae had to learn how to accept it or be in for the greatest disappointment of their life.

"Yeah, I'm sure. Go."

"I'm so sorry," Julie said, even as she drew away. "I'll call you after?"

Rae gave her an uncomfortable smile, not quite willing to say yes, but not wanting to say no either. And from the resigned expression on Julie's face, she'd noticed Rae's reluctance.

"I'm sorry," she said one more time, and with that, she turned and walked away.

ELEVEN

JULIE

JULIE STOOD at the foot of the hospital bed where her patient was unconscious and on a ventilator. She was stable now, but it had taken Julie's entire team hours to bring her back from the brink. Technically, she had died. Had been dead for a couple of minutes. Now it was just a waiting game to see when she would wake up—*if* she would wake up.

The infant was doing better. He was premature and would have to spend at least a month in the NICU, but he wasn't in any immediate danger.

Viola walked in quietly and came to stand next to Julie. She didn't speak. She didn't need to. They'd both been in this game long enough to know that no words would make this situation any easier.

Cases like these were always the most difficult: when the outcome was still so uncertain and there was no closure. No celebration because the patient would recover. Nothing to mourn either. Everyone was left in limbo with no concrete answers for family members who were desperate for them.

Silently, they left the room and slipped into the staff lounge, collapsing onto the couches.

"You can let the family in to see her. I've already explained her condition to them." Julie's voice sounded flat, drained, devoid of life.

Viola nodded. "You should go home."

"I can stay." The words came out before Julie could stop them. She hated going home during times like these. She understood there wasn't anything she could do that hadn't already been done. But sitting at home, stewing while staring at the wall was so much worse. At least at the hospital, there was always a distraction waiting just around the corner.

Viola glanced over at her and Julie could feel the weight of her judgment without even looking up.

"If you don't want to go home, then go somewhere else. Go see that hottie team captain of yours."

Julie tried to scowl at Viola, but she suspected it looked more like a pout. Ever since Rae had delivered flowers to the ward, Viola had been teasing her non-stop. It was good-natured and gentle, and Julie was more shy about it than annoyed. She'd admitted that she found Rae attractive, but she hadn't had a chance to tell Viola about Rae spending the night last night.

"Why are you making that face?" Viola asked, looking slightly alarmed.

"I'm not making a face." Julie tried to school her expression, but Viola wasn't that easily fooled.

"Did something happen between you and the hottie team captain?" Viola leaned over and poked Julie lightly in the arm.

Julie opened her mouth, then shut it again. Her first instinct was to say no, but there was no point in hiding the truth from Viola. Not when everything inside her lit up at the memory. Rae's lips on her skin, their fingers inside her body, the way they moved around her kitchen, the roguish smile that made Julie's heart skip a beat.

Viola pinned her with an interrogating look. "Doctor Julia Chan, have you been holding out on me?"

"It was just last night," Julie hissed back at her.

Viola cocked an eyebrow. "And? How was it?"

Julie's cheeks, ears, and neck all heated with an aggressive blush. "It was good," she said in a small voice, almost afraid she would jinx herself if she spoke too loud.

As wonderful as last night had been, she wasn't sure where she stood with Rae after this morning. They had not been pleased when Julie ran off before practice even began, and Julie was torn between wanting to call Rae to hear their voice again and afraid Rae wouldn't even bother answering the phone.

A part of Julie didn't even blame them. School, then work, had always been her most important concern, and she'd structured her life around excelling at both. To the point where she didn't have space for much else. Making it to dragon boat practices on time was already a challenge, what did she have left to give to Rae?

The question was, was she willing to change for Rae? Could she reshuffle the priorities that had guided her for so long? Julie didn't know the answer to that question. She didn't even know which answer she wanted to be true.

"Well, then, you should go see them," Viola said with all the confidence Julie didn't feel. "Seriously. Go. Shoo. Get out of here."

Viola stood and pulled Julie to her feet before hustling her off toward the staff lockers. Too tired to argue, Julie moved on autopilot, her hands and feet going through the motions of grabbing her things and walking out of the hospital.

Her mind bounced back and forth between Rae and the surgery. What would Rae say if Julie called them? How upset would they be? Had there been a misstep during the emergency cesarean? Was there anything else Julie could have done?

Preoccupied, Julie didn't remember getting on the streetcar or getting off and walking the few blocks to her apartment. She didn't remember going up the elevator or pulling her keys out to unlock the door. Only after it snicked shut behind her did she come back to herself. She dropped her bag on the floor and slumped back against the wall.

Her eyes slid shut as the adrenaline in her system finally wore off. Overcome by fatigue, she almost fell asleep right there, sitting on the floor.

The sound of her phone buzzing jolted her from her semi-consciousness. Her pulse raced as she scrambled for her phone. Could it be the hospital? Did something happen with her patient?

When she finally found her phone and saw the name on the caller ID, tears welled up in her eyes. It was Rae.

"Hello?" She didn't care if she sounded too eager. She wanted to hear Rae's voice. She wanted Rae to tell her everything was going to be okay.

"Hey, uh, is this a good time?"

Suddenly, it felt both like the weight of the world had lifted off her shoulders and also like she was falling apart, all at the same time. "Yeah," she croaked. "I just got home."

Tears spilled down her cheeks, and her legs flopped out in front of her like a rag doll.

"Are you okay?" Rae sounded cautious and concerned.

A slightly hysterical laugh gurgled up in Julie, sounding more like a sob than anything else. "I—" *Fine* was poised on the tip of her tongue, but she stopped herself.

Technically, she was fine. Or at least, she would be. But right now, at this very moment, she was anything but fine. She was tired. Exhausted. Not just physically, but emotionally too.

But she'd always been so strong, so driven, an over-achiever who excelled at everything she put her hand to. So much so that everyone she knew assumed she had it all under control. They expected her to be fine, and she never gave them any reason to think otherwise.

Except Rae. Rae judged her. Rae saw the ways she

was deficient and wasn't afraid to call her out on them. Rae understood that her success came with consequences, and they cared enough to point them out. It was an uncomfortable feeling, having someone break through her carefully constructed exterior. But it was also a relief, knowing she didn't have to pretend to be perfect all the time.

"I don't know," Julie finally answered.

A beat passed in silence before Rae spoke. "Tell me."

Julie dropped her head into her hand. It felt too heavy for her neck to hold up. "I don't know where to start."

"Your patient. How is she doing?" Rae's voice was steady and grounding, a firm foundation Julie could rest on.

"She's... alive. For now. She lost a lot of blood during surgery. We don't know if she'll wake up." Julie winced at the sound of her own voice: detached, cold, clinical. She didn't mean to sound like that. But sometimes, that was the only way she could get through it—pretend it was a case study from a textbook rather than a real human she had under her scalpel.

"Shit." No empty words of comfort. No false optimism. Rae's easy acknowledgment and acceptance of the situation was a balm to Julie's weathered spirit.

"Yeah."

Another beat of silence passed, and Rae didn't try to fill it. It stretched until something snapped inside Julie, and it all came spilling out.

"I love what I do," she said as big, unwieldy feelings

surged through her. "I know it sounds silly, but it's not just a job to me. It's who I am. I can't imagine myself not being a doctor. It's the only thing I've ever wanted to do with my life. But sometimes... sometimes, it's just so hard and I'm so tired and—" She cut herself off and held her breath to keep a wretched sob from escaping her throat.

She'd spent her entire life keeping her shit together and pushing through whatever obstacles stood in her way. And now, faced with Rae's uncanny ability to break through her defenses, Julie was suddenly desperate to let it all fall apart.

She wanted to be a messy disaster and not worry about how it would be perceived by others. She wanted to let it all go, let the cards fall where they may, and be the kind of flawed human being everyone else managed to get away with. But she battled against herself, the decades of self-imposed rigidity rising up and resisting. She was caught in the middle, pulled in opposite directions, and torn down the middle.

"Julie?"

She didn't trust herself to speak. "Hmm?"

"I'm coming over."

Her first instinct was to turn Rae down, to deny she wanted to see them. But she couldn't make the words form on her tongue. She *did* want to see Rae. With a wretchedness she could feel clawing at her insides. She craved the safety and strength of Rae's arms holding her tight. The way they could chase away the rest of the world and protect her.

Still... "Are you sure?"

"Yes, I'm sure."

Julie felt the warmth of Rae's words travel all the way through the phone line, and she clung to that feeling like her life depended upon it.

"Hold on, babe, I'm on my way."

TWELVE

RAE

RAE BRACED themself the entire journey to Julie's apartment. They weren't entirely sure what they would find there. Julie was in distress, that much was clear. But to what degree? And what, if anything, could Rae do about it?

Rae knocked on Julie's door and there was a scraping, fumbling sound on the other side before the lock flipped and the handle turned. As it opened, it sounded like there was something heavy being pushed out of the way at the same time.

Julie stood in the doorway, still wearing her pink scrubs and running shoes. Most of her hair had fallen out of her ponytail, and there were dark smudges under her eyes.

She looked like death warmed over. And Rae had never seen anyone so beautiful before.

"Thank you. Sorry." She stepped to the side to let Rae slip in.

Behind the door was a giant canvas tote bag with papers, napkins, wrappers, a water bottle, a stethoscope, and a bunch of other random things spilling out. It looked like Julie had dropped it the second she'd gotten home and hadn't bothered to pick it up again.

"Come here." Rae drew her into their arms and she melted against them. A few moments later, moisture seeped through the fabric of Rae's shirt as Julie cried silent tears.

Rae's heart ached for Julie. She was a strong woman. She was ambitious, high-achieving, and a hard worker. But no one could be strong all the time. Everyone had moments of vulnerability, times when their strength ran out. When did that happen for Julie? And who did she have who could pick her up again?

They wanted to be that person for Julie. The one who took care of her when she couldn't take care of herself. Who protected her when others asked too much of her. Rae wanted to be the one Julie depended upon when so many others depended on her.

Rae guided her to the couch and they laid down on it together, Julie tucked safely between their body and the couch cushions. They held her like that, neither speaking, just dwelling in the comfort of being together, the knowledge that they weren't alone. Gradually, the tension in Julie's body melted away, her breathing grew deeper, and her limbs became lax.

"Babe?" Rae whispered, but there was no answer.

The sun creeped down toward the horizon, painting

the sky blue and purple and pink. Minutes turned into an hour. Only then did Julie stir.

She moaned and lifted a hand to rub her eyes. "I fell asleep?"

"Mmhmm."

"Sorry." She awkwardly pushed herself up to sitting and Rae reluctantly let her go.

"Don't be. You were tired."

Head bowed, Julie dropped her hand into her lap, shoulders slumped forward. Every breath she took appeared labored. Every movement looked pained.

Her stomach gurgled loudly, and Rae didn't know whether to laugh or groan.

"When's the last time you ate?" they asked, untangling themself from Julie and standing to their feet.

Julie's brow furrowed in thought. "Um... maybe breakfast?"

Rae rolled their eyes. "Why am I not surprised?"

Julie cast them a sheepish smile.

"Come on. I think I saw a bag of frozen dumplings in your freezer." Rae pulled Julie off the couch and directed her toward the kitchen.

Rae filled a pot of water and set it to boil, then dug out the half full bag of dumplings. They were pretty frostbitten, and the skins would most likely tear while boiling, emptying all the filling into the water. But it was better than nothing—better than ordering take out.

Julie sat at the kitchen island, watching Rae work, and just like yesterday, the domesticity of the scene struck a chord in Rae. It was so comfortable. It felt so right. Rae could see themself like this, cooking for Julie, for a good long time.

"Thank you," Julie finally spoke after an extended period of pleasant silence. "For coming over. Today was rough."

Rae glanced over as they stirred the pot of boiling dumplings. "Do they happen often?"

Julie's shoulder twitched in a shrug. "Some cases hit me harder than others."

"What do you normally do when that happens?" Rae had a feeling they weren't going to like the answer, but they still had to ask.

It took Julie a few moments to reply. "Normally... I ignore it and push through."

Rae winced. "That doesn't sound super healthy."

"No," Julie said with a resigned sigh. "I suppose it doesn't."

"Do you ever take vacations?" Rae turned the burner off and pulled a large bowl from the cupboard.

Julie didn't respond, so Rae turned to see if she'd heard the question. She was giving them an incredulous look. "Vacation? I don't even know what that word means."

They shook their head in disapproval. "Vacation. You know, when you take time off work to relax, do something fun, maybe get away."

Julie sighed. "Does helping my parents move back to Hong Kong count?"

Rae gave her a look of skepticism. "Probably not. When was that anyway?"

Her head tilted, gaze drifting up to the ceiling as she thought. "Maybe seven years ago?"

Rae groaned. "Seriously? Babe, you need to take a vacation. A long one."

Julie laughed, the sound high and bright, winding its way through Rae and ensnaring them.

They brought the bowl of dumplings over to the island and set it in front of Julie, along with a spoon and a bottle of soy sauce.

"You're not having any?" Julie asked when she saw there was only enough for one serving.

Rae shook their head. "I already ate at home."

Julie smiled, sweet and shy, and Rae leaned in to plant a quick kiss on the corner of her mouth. They watched as Julie gobbled down the food, and all the appreciative sounds she made filled Rae with a sense of pride and accomplishment, even though all they did was boil some water.

After Julie was finished, Rae cleaned up the kitchen, then led Julie toward the bedroom.

The en suite bathroom was equipped with a walk-in shower as well as a free-standing soaking tub. Rae plugged the drain on the bathtub and cranked the hot water.

"I don't remember the last time I had a bath," Julie commented from her spot leaning against the door frame.

"You should do it more often." Digging under the sink, they found a container of Epsom salts and dumped a generous amount into the filling tub. The smell of lilacs filled the air as the scented Epsom salts dissolved into the water.

"It's not as efficient as a shower."

Rae turned and threw a mock scowl in her direction. "It's not always about efficiency."

Julie's lips twitched in amusement. Rae approached, and she straightened, peering up at them through her lashes. They pushed the stray strands of hair out of her face and felt their heart somersault in their chest. This woman... this beautiful, intelligent, determined woman. Rae wanted to wrap her up in the softest blankets and protect her from everything and everyone—herself included.

Julie turned her face into Rae's palm, eyes drifting shut as she took comfort in the small touch. Her lashes were dark against cheeks ashen from fatigue. She sighed, letting the weight of her head settle into Rae's hand.

They'd been wary of this relationship with Julie, and perhaps they still had reason to be. But despite all the warning signs posted along the way and the alarm bells ringing overhead, Rae had forged ahead. And now... now, it was too late to turn around. Julie had found her way into Rae's life and heart, and there wasn't much they could do about it except continue on.

"Will you be okay taking a bath on your own?"

The corners of Julie's lips turned down into a sheepish pout. "No?"

Rae tilted their head in question.

"I'd... I'd rather you take it with me?"

Heat immediately bloomed across Rae's stomach and down to their groin. Swallowing down a growl, they fought the urge to rip Julie's clothes from her body and devour her whole. They cleared their throat before speaking, but even then, the words came out thick with desire. "Yeah, I can do that."

Stepping back, Rae adverted their eyes as they quickly stripped down and stepped into the tub. When they sank below the hot water and turned back to Julie, they forgot to breathe.

All that soft, flawless skin. Dark nipples plump and begging to be sucked. The shadow of neatly trimmed hair between her legs. Rae stared, riveted, as Julie approached. They spread their legs to make room for her, and a tremor of pleasure raced through them as Julie fitted herself against Rae's body.

They wasted no time in filling their hands with the rounded curves of Julie's hips, the flatness of her stomach, the hefty weight of her breasts. Julie leaned her head back on Rae's shoulder, exposing the elegant length of her neck, the delicate line of her collarbone. She rested her arms on top of Rae's, laced her fingers between theirs, and guided one down, deep into the water.

Rae found the swollen nub of Julie's clit easily, and a couple rubs was all they needed to make Julie's breath catch. Then down, even farther, into the folds of Julie's pussy. Julie tilted her hips and Rae's fingers slid inside, two at once—hot, tight, quivering, and tender.

Rae licked along Julie's neck, found the place where

her pulse was the strongest, and felt it race beneath their lips. They squeezed Julie's breast, pinched the nipple, and pulled on it until Julie let out a soft cry.

Fuck, she was so responsive, so sensitive. Every touch, every kiss, Julie reacted like she was a finely tuned instrument and Rae a freaking maestro.

Holding Julie tightly, they shifted their hips, rubbing their pelvis up against Julie's ass. Their clit throbbed from the friction as pleasure built inside them.

Inside Julie, their fingers curled, pressing against the bundle of nerves concentrated there. They ground the heel of their hand against Julie's clit. Alternating back and forth, they kept up the pressure as Julie's cries grew louder and louder in their ear.

"Rae!" She gripped their wrists tightly, holding them in place. Her body twisted and jerked in Rae's arms. Then suddenly, her thighs slammed together, trapping Rae's hand between them, her body went taut, head thrown back, and she let out a low, soul-shaking groan.

Not far behind, Rae rubbed themself against Julie's body. Their nipples tingled against Julie's back, their clit ached with the need for release. Julie's pussy pulsed around their fingers as if it were trying to suck them in deeper. Pressing their face against Julie's neck, they came in shuttering, mind-bending waves of pleasure.

They sat like that, catching their breaths, until the water started growing cold. Reluctantly, they got out and toweled off, then slid into the bed together, still naked.

Rae gathered her to them.

"Thank you again," Julie whispered. "No one's ever taken care of me like this before."

Rae gave her a gentle kiss on the forehead, their heart aching for Julie. "Well, you have me now."

THIRTEEN

JULIE

JULIE PLACED a reassuring hand on the shoulder of the pregnant woman lying on the stretcher. "Hang tight, we'll get you admitted upstairs as soon as possible."

Arms wrapped around her belly, the patient tried to smile at her, but it came across more like a grimace. She was in pain, but Julie was hesitant to up her medication any higher than it already was for fear of causing harm to the fetus.

"Thank you," the patient's partner mumbled as Julie slipped out of the curtained area around the bed.

As she pulled the curtain closed behind her, a paramedic team rolled in with a patient on the opposite side of the Emergency Room.

Julie did a double take. It was hard to mistake the undercut and the arms of colorful tattoos. But the sight was so foreign and unexpected, it took her a moment to fully comprehend what she was seeing. She rushed over.

"Rae?"

Rae's head jerked up, eyes wide with fear, and lips pressed firmly together as if they were fighting to stay composed. Their body was tense, shoulders raised, muscles so taut they were trembling. The second recognition set in, Rae's expression turned desperate, pleading.

"Rae, what happened?" Julie's emergency training kicked in as she fell into step with the paramedics who were wheeling the stretcher into an empty examination bay.

"She— She fell—"

Julie glanced down at the patient, and her stomach sank. PoPo lay there, face pale and eyes fluttering as if she was trying to open them, but didn't have the strength. Her brows were furrowed, and she breathed heavily, indicating obvious pain.

A paramedic took over when Rae couldn't get the words out. "Patient is female, eighty-two, history of osteoporosis and type-two diabetes. She fell from standing height and injured her left hip. We've stabilized and iced and administered five milligrams of morphine."

"Transfer on my count, one, two, three," an ER nurse counted out loud and the team lifted PoPo from the ambulance's stretcher to the hospital's gurney. She then looked to Julie, eyebrow cocked in question. "Are you taking this patient, Doctor Chan?"

"Oh, no, I'm..." Julie's tongue stumbled over what exactly Rae was to her, and her cheeks warmed in response. "I'm a friend of the family."

If the nurse picked up on Julie's awkwardness, she

ignored it. Instead, she nodded perfunctorily. "The doctor will be by shortly."

"Thank you," Julie replied as she pushed Rae down into a chair.

It said volumes that Rae didn't resist her and only scooted the chair closer to the bed to hold PoPo's hand.

"Is she...?" Rae's voice trailed off, but Julie didn't need them to finish the question. It was one she got every single day.

"We'll know more once they take some x-rays." She stood behind the chair and laid her hand on Rae's shoulder. "Can you tell me what happened?"

Rae shook their head as if in denial. "I went to visit her and the receptionist at the front desk said she was in her room. I found her on the floor. I don't know how long she'd been lying there." Rae's voice broke in a sob, and they covered their mouth with a hand.

The pain in Rae's voice broke Julie's heart. It was the same pain she'd heard so many times from the loved ones of patients—driven by guilt, amplified by fear, and made all the worse because there was so little they could do. As a doctor, Julie had told herself she was used to hearing it, that it didn't affect her anymore. But standing next to Rae, she knew that was a lie—it would always affect her.

"I should have gotten there sooner," Rae said softly, more to themself than anyone else. "If I had just gone straight from home instead of running all those errands, I would've gotten there earlier. I could've prevented this. This is my fault."

Julie crouched down in front of Rae, turning them

away from the bed and bracketing their face with her hands. She couldn't let them go down that path, not when they'd done absolutely nothing wrong.

"Rae, look at me. This isn't your fault. I know it feels that way, and your brain will come up with a dozen scenarios for how you could have prevented this from happening. But you couldn't have prevented it. If PoPo hadn't fallen today, she could have fallen tomorrow or the day after or next week. Seniors fall all the time."

Rae shook their head. "You weren't there. You didn't see her lying on the floor. I thought she was dead at first. I thought I'd lost her."

"But you didn't. She's still here. PoPo's a fighter, and we're going to do everything we can to help her."

"But..." Rae's eyes were watery with unshed tears as they stared at Julie. "It's serious, isn't it? When seniors fall?"

Julie hesitated. Based on the location of the injury and how much pain PoPo was in, Julie wouldn't be surprised if she fractured her hip. And seniors were at increased risk of complications with that kind of injury. But Julie didn't know for sure, and it would be ethically irresponsible of her to start giving medical opinions without the necessary tests to support them.

But Rae was looking at her with such pleading in their eyes, desperate for answers, for reassurance. Julie couldn't not give it to them, not when they'd already done so much for her.

"It could be. We won't know for sure until the scans

are back. But if it's a fractured hip, she could need a hip replacement, and recovery will be long and difficult."

"But she *will* recover?"

Julie wanted to say yes, of course, Rae had nothing to worry about, but she couldn't. That wouldn't be fair. "Many do. Some don't. The key is to get them back on their feet quickly. The longer they spend immobile, the worse the outcomes are."

Julie watched, stomach sinking, as whatever color that remained in Rae's face drained away completely. She hated that she was the cause of this reaction, that she couldn't tell Rae everything would turn out okay.

But then Rae closed their eyes and took a deep breath. When they looked up again, there was a steeliness in their gaze that reminded Julie of the first day they'd met. Rae sat up straighter, ferocity and determination shining from their eyes.

They stood, pushing the chair back with a loud scraping sound. "Where's the doctor?"

Julie stood with them. "Someone will come by as soon as they're available."

They pinned her with an expression that bordered on a scowl. "You're a doctor. You work here. Can't you order the tests or whatever?"

Technically, she could, but this wasn't her area of expertise. Julie let out an apologetic sigh. "Let me see if they can squeeze you in."

She left Rae at PoPo's bedside and found one of the ER nurses. "Hey, is Doctor Chopra from orthopedics in today?"

The nurse paused in the middle of whatever she was doing and gave Julie a very unimpressed look. Her gaze flicked to Julie's badge hanging around her neck, and Julie could see her debating whether she should push back against the demanding doctor who didn't even work in the ER.

"Please?" she added, offering the nurse a contrite smile. "My friend's grandmother most likely has a fractured hip and we'd like to get her off your hands as quickly as possible."

The nurse sighed and tapped on a touch screen that was connected to the hospital's communication system. "Yes, Doctor Chopra is working today. Would you like me to page her for you?"

"That would be amazing. Thank you so much."

"You're welcome," the nurse replied, not sounding the least bit generous.

When Julie returned to PoPo's bed, she found Rae bent over their grandmother, carefully brushing her hair away from her face. PoPo moaned quietly and grimaced in pain. Her lashes fluttered before her eyes opened just a slit.

"Rae," she said, voice hoarse, barely audible.

"I'm here, PoPo. I'm right here. We're at the hospital. Everything's going to be okay. I promise." To a stranger, Rae's voice would've sounded confident and self-assured, but Julie detected a slight waver at the end that betrayed their fear and anxiety.

She curled her hands into fists and stuffed them into the pockets of her doctor's coat. The first lesson she'd learned as an intern at the hospital was to never promise anything. Routine surgeries could have unforeseen complications. Patients who should have died miraculously pulled through. Nothing was ever guaranteed.

But Julie vowed to herself that she would do everything in her power to make sure PoPo was taken care of. She would do everything she could to help Rae keep their word.

FOURTEEN

RAE

WALKING into PoPo's room earlier that day was one of the worst moments in Rae's life. Their normally upbeat, teasing, and lively grandmother had been sprawled on the floor, semiconscious, unable to move, unable even to shout for help. Rae had dropped the flowers and bags of fruit they'd brought and rushed to her side, but they hadn't known if PoPo could recognize them, she'd been so out of it.

They were furious. At the long-term care staff for not finding PoPo before they did. At themself for not getting there earlier. At PoPo for not being more careful. At the world for trying to take away the one person in the world that Rae had left.

More than the anger, though, Rae had been terrified.

Fear had gripped them during the wait for the ambulance and all through the ride to the hospital. Only when they saw Julie in the Emergency Room did they feel like they could breathe again. But that relief didn't last long.

PoPo's hip was broken. A femoral neck fracture, they called it. And given PoPo's history of osteoporosis and her age, Dr. Chopra recommended a total hip replacement.

Rae didn't like the sound of that. It felt like a lot, extreme, risky. Wouldn't it be safer to do something less invasive than cut out huge chunks of bone and replace it with metal and plastic?

Julie had tried to explain it. A partial replacement would be less invasive and typically had shorter recovery times. But that kind of hip prothesis also had greater contact with bone and cartilage, which could aggravate PoPo's osteoporosis and require more surgeries in the future.

They'd given Rae some pamphlets that laid out the pros and cons of each, but the more Rae read, the more confused they got. There was no obvious answer. No option that was definitely better than the other. Rae hated that kind of uncertainty, hated that they were essentially gambling with their grandmother's life. What if they made the wrong decision? What if PoPo never recovered from surgery? What if she died?

Rae wouldn't be able to live with themself.

Dr. Chopra had upped PoPo's morphine. It made her a little dopey, but at least it managed the pain enough for PoPo to speak. Not that she was much help. She'd put on a brave face when Dr. Chopra was explaining the options, saying she was good with whatever Rae thought was best. But Rae could see the fear hiding just behind her bravado.

PoPo had always been so strong, so capable. She raised Rae all by herself, working well past retirement age to make sure Rae was provided for. Laid out in the hospital bed, covered in the thin, white sheet and rough blue blanket, PoPo looked so small and fragile—nothing like the commanding woman Rae had grown up with.

In the end, they'd opted for the total hip replacement, even though it felt like they were flipping a coin on their grandmother's life. And now, PoPo was in surgery while Rae paced around the waiting room, practically crawling out of their skin.

From her spot in the corner, Julie glanced up from her iPad where she was updating patient charts, and watched as Rae turned circles in the room. She hadn't budged from Rae's side since the moment PoPo had been wheeled into the Emergency Room, even though she was still technically at work. A part of Rae felt bad about keeping Julie away from her responsibilities; but another part—the bigger part—couldn't have cared less. They'd needed Julie, and for once, she was there.

Julie set her iPad aside and rose from her seat, stretching as she crossed into Rae's path. Rae stopped and let themself be drawn into a hug. They clung to Julie, unable to fully relax into the embrace.

"I hate this waiting," they murmured. Dr. Chopra said the surgery would take about two hours, and they were half an hour past that already. Every minute felt like a decade.

"I know." Julie rubbed a comforting hand up and

down their back. "Do you want me to go ask for an update?"

Before they could respond, Dr. Chopra appeared in the doorway. Rae stiffened, bracing themself, not sure if they wanted to hear what Dr. Chopra had to say. If it was bad news, wouldn't it be better to put it off for as long as humanly possible?

Next to them, Julie had her hand on their back, and Rae leaned into her touch, drawing on her strength.

Dr. Chopra gave them a reserved smile. "We just finished the surgery, and your grandmother is being taken to recovery. It took a little longer than we had anticipated, but everything went according to plan. You should be able to see her soon."

Rae's heart hammered in their chest, and air rushed out of their lungs from the breath they'd been holding. Relief flooded their system, making their knees weak. Julie caught them as they sank into the closest chair.

Tears sprung to their eyes and escaped down their cheeks. They'd managed not to cry during this entire ordeal, keeping a tight rein on their emotions so they could focus on PoPo. But now, hearing that PoPo had come through the surgery successfully, all the feelings Rae hadn't allowed themself to feel came pouring out.

Bone-deep and terrifying, the realization that they could have been left alone in the world was far scarier than they'd ever imagined. PoPo had been their anchor, the one person they knew they could count on, no matter what. Even when she moved into the long-term care home, PoPo was never more than a phone call away, always armed with advice and encouragement.

And Rae had come so close to losing her.

Her words from weeks ago echoed through Rae's mind. *I won't be here forever. I don't want you to be alone.* At the time, Rae had dismissed her concerns, but now, Rae understood why she'd said them.

Life was fragile. It was unpredictable. You never knew what tomorrow would bring. So, why wait?

Julie held them, murmuring soft words as Rae tried to pull themself together.

"We already have her scheduled in with the physical therapist," Dr. Chopra continued when Rae finally managed to calm down. "And as long as everything progresses as expected, we should be able to discharge her in a couple of days."

"Thank you. Thank you so much," Rae said. Those words were insufficient to capture the depth of gratitude they felt.

Dr. Chopra smiled understandingly. "You're very welcome. I'm glad we could help your grandmother."

"Can I see her?" Rae asked, wanting to be there when she awoke. She'd probably be disoriented, and Rae didn't want her to feel scared or alone.

Dr. Chopra nodded. "Yes, of course. She should be in recovery by now. Can you take them?" she directed the last question to Julie.

"Yeah, I've got it."

When Rae finally felt steady enough to walk, Julie

led them through the hallways of the hospital and into the recovery ward.

PoPo was still asleep from the anesthesia when Rae stepped up to the bed. She was so still, utterly motionless, save for the slight rise and fall of her chest. An oxygen mask covered her mouth and nose, and tubes snaked out from her body, connecting her to various machines.

Rae placed one hand on PoPo's forehead and the other on her shoulder. The warmth under their palms was reassuring, a sign that PoPo was alive, that she could recover.

"When will she wake up?"

Julie stood at the foot of the bed. "It's just a matter of time before the anesthesia wears off. It's different for each person, but it shouldn't take too long."

Rae's brain started skipping ahead to all the things they would need to do to help PoPo during her recovery. She would need more support for simple life tasks like going to the washroom and taking showers. Daily physical therapy sessions and individual exercises on top of that. Rae wasn't sure they could rely on the staff at the long-term care home to step up. Which meant they would need to do it—on top of the flower shop and dragon boat.

And Julie.

Maybe. Perhaps.

PoPo wanted to see them settled, and for the first time in their life, Rae understood why. The question was, was Julie the right person to settle down with?

Julie came around the side of the bed and slipped her

arms around Rae's waist. She propped her chin on Rae's shoulder, pressing their bodies together until Rae relaxed into her embrace.

In their heart of hearts, they knew Julie was the person for them. If they weren't already half in love with her, then they were well on their way. But love wasn't always enough, and Rae didn't know if Julie would be able to meet them halfway.

FIFTEEN

JULIE

FIFTEEN HOURS after Rae and PoPo arrived at the hospital, Julie finally managed to convince Rae to go home for a shower, some sleep, and a bite of food. PoPo had woken up, still groggy and a little disoriented, and she would be in and out of sleep for the rest of the night. There was no point in Rae staying in the hospital when they could be sleeping in their own bed.

They lived in a semi-detached house just off the Danforth on the east end of the city. The ground floor had a big bay window in the front and a walkout to a small backyard. It had a warm, bohemian feel with brightly colored walls, mismatched furniture, and plants tucked into every nook and cranny. The entire place was Rae personified.

Julie followed Rae into the living room area where they dropped wordlessly into an armchair. Slumped low, legs sprawled out in front of them, Rae dropped their head back to stare unseeingly up at the ceiling.

Julie knew the feeling. It was the type of fatigue that sank deep into the bone, smothering every thought, zapping every ounce of strength. So potent, it stole a person's ability to sleep and turned them into a living zombie.

She brushed her fingers through strands of Rae's hair and cupped her palm against their cheek. Their own hand drifted up to cover Julie's, and their eyes drifted shut with a sigh.

"You okay?" Julie asked, rubbing her thumb back and forth across Rae's cheekbone.

Rae blinked slowly, breathed even slower, but eventually shifted their gaze up toward Julie.

Her breath caught in her throat at the raw emotion she saw in Rae's eyes. Fear, hope, worry, longing, each one distinct yet amplified by the others. They held her, ensnared, and Julie felt herself getting lost in their depths.

Rae moved in slow motion, rising to their feet and drawing Julie in close. Their arm snaked around Julie's waist, drawing her flush against their body.

Julie gasped as heat shot right through her, pooling between her legs. She sighed when Rae captured her lips in a kiss.

It started soft and gentle but quickly grew urgent and hungry. Rae thrust their tongue into her mouth, bit down on her bottom lip, and bent her backward to angle her the way they wanted. Julie surrendered, opening herself up to Rae, to be used however they needed.

Their hands roamed. One slid down to Julie's ass,

gripping it tight before hiking Julie's leg up around their hip. The other slipped under the hem of Julie's shirt and rose to cup Julie's breast, kneading it through her bra. They kissed their way down her neck, then back up to nibble on her earlobe.

Her head swam with desire, and her body trembled with arousal. Everywhere Rae touched burned with a fire that threatened to consume her.

Rae grabbed the hem of her shirt, and in one fluid motion, pulled it over her head. Julie followed their lead, unsnapping her bra and shoving her pants down past her thighs. Their clothes flew, landing all over the living room, and the second they were both naked again, they came back together.

Rae shuffled Julie backward until her legs hit the edge of the couch, and they both tumbled down onto the cushions. Flat on her back, Julie was at their mercy.

They trailed their mouth down to capture one nipple, then the other, sucking the delicate flesh between their lips, swirling their tongue around the sensitive bud.

Then farther still, down Julie's stomach, all the way to her pussy. Rae pushed her legs apart, lifting one up over their shoulder. Then they scooted in close until their wetness met Julie's.

She gasped as their most intimate parts touched. A whimper escaped when Rae rubbed themself against her, followed by a cry when they reached out and pinched a nipple between their fingers.

Above her, Rae loomed large, strands of hair falling into their face and their makeup smudged around their eyes, making them look dangerous and intimidating. Their dragon boat-toned body undulated, rolling from stomach to chest to shoulders. Like a deity had come down from the heavens to ride Julie's body and take whatever they desired.

Julie's hands found their way to Rae's hips, helping them find just the right rhythm that would drive them both toward orgasms. It didn't take long. With the vision of Rae in front of them and the friction of Rae's pussy against hers, it was only moments before pleasure crested and crashed. Coming hard, her grip on Rae's hips tightened until she was afraid she'd leave marks.

Half a second later, Rae, too, came with a shout, jerking themself against Julie to milk every last ounce of pleasure from both of their bodies.

Eventually exhausted, Rae collapsed on top of Julie, and she welcomed their weight. Tucking their head under her chin, she held them tight as they both caught their breaths. Julie was drifting, semiconscious, when Rae stirred.

"Thank you," they murmured against her neck.

"You don't have to thank me," she replied, feeling entirely undeserving of Rae's gratitude.

"I don't know what I would've done if you hadn't been at the hospital." Their fingers started to move, tracing invisible patterns across Julie's shoulder.

"You would've been amazing," Julie reassured them. "You would've advocated for PoPo and gotten her the best treatment available."

"Still. I'm glad you were there."

Julie gave Rae a kiss on the top of their head, her heart swelling until it felt too big for her chest. "I'm glad I was there too."

After the sweat had cooled on their skin, Rae lifted themself off Julie, then helped her to her feet. They led the way upstairs to the bathroom where they showered together. Soapy hands covered every inch of skin. Their mouths met in lazy, wet kisses. It was intimate and worshipful, two souls finding comfort in each other, taking and giving as each needed.

After the shower, they slid in between the sheets, curling themselves around each other. It wasn't long before Rae fell asleep, but Julie remained wide awake, staring at the wall.

She had a sneaking suspicion she was in love with Rae. The way they were so willing to take care of her. How devoted they were to PoPo. The passion they had for dragon boat and the community they'd built there. The success of their flower store. Rae was an incredible person who Julie felt honored to know. That such a person would care about Julie was humbling—and scary. She didn't know if she could live up to it, if she could give Rae what they deserved.

They deserved someone who would make them a priority, someone who didn't have competing demands on their time. But Julie had been clear from the start that her work would always come first. She was a doctor—it wasn't merely a job to her, it was her calling, it was who she was. Until she met Rae, she had never contemplated being anything else.

But now... maybe there was another way to be a doctor, a way that didn't require her to work such long shifts or be at the beck and call of the hospital. Maybe she could find a way to fulfill her calling while also building a life with Rae.

Do you ever take vacations?

Rae's question had been haunting her ever since they'd asked it. No, historically, Julie didn't take vacations. She wasn't even sure how many vacation days she was entitled to. Could she take a few? Perhaps a week to unwind and reset?

The idea was so foreign to her, it actually sounded a little scary. Julie laughed silently at herself. Wow, she was pathetic. Afraid of taking a week off work because she wouldn't know what to do with herself. If she couldn't handle a little vacation, how would she ever be able to make bigger, lasting changes?

She didn't have the answer to that. And she didn't know how long it would take her to figure it out.

Was that fair to Rae? Asking them to stick around while she sorted her life out? Probably not.

With sleep eluding her, Julie carefully eased herself out of Rae's embrace. The loss of warmth was immediate, sending chills right down to the depths of her soul. In bare feet and wearing one of Rae's t-shirts that hung down to mid-thigh, she padded downstairs and dug her phone out of her tote bag. She checked to see if she'd missed any messages from the hospital and breathed a sigh of relief when there were none.

She wandered into the kitchen, peeking into the

cupboards and shelves, marveling at all the ingredients she didn't recognize. The kitchen was stocked fuller than a grocery store, but the one thing Julie didn't find was coffee.

The closest she got was a container of the cheap instant stuff. Offended, she debated throwing the whole thing out. Instead, she pulled up an app on her phone and placed an order for some real coffee, throwing in a bag of beans at the same time. And while she waited, she placed a second order for a decent coffee maker for Rae.

SIXTEEN

RAE

POPO WAS DISCHARGED from the hospital four days after her surgery, and Rae spent the better part of every day since at the long-term care home with her. She started physical therapy almost immediately, with daily visits from the physical therapist. To say that PoPo disliked the exercises was the understatement of the decade, but Rae wasn't about to let her complaining derail her own recovery. They'd read that one of the biggest challenges when it came to seniors with hip replacements was being too sedentary, losing muscle mass, and increasing the risk of future falls.

At The Flower Shoppe, Raufikat had been nothing short of a lifesaver, working more hours and taking over some of Rae's responsibilities. They'd even brought on a part-time high school student to help alleviate the workload.

Now, two weeks later, it felt like they were finally getting a grasp on things. Rae wasn't gripped with terror every time PoPo tried to move about on her own. PoPo had been able to pare back her pain medication. The long-term care home had assigned staff to check in on PoPo more frequently.

The only thing was Julie.

With Julie's typically busy work schedule and every spare minute of Rae's time funneled into caring for PoPo, they hadn't seen each other outside of dragon boat practices. They exchanged text messages every day and tried to connect over the phone. But despite PoPo's accident having brought them closer together, it now felt like they were drifting farther apart.

It was frustrating, but there wasn't much Rae could do about it. They'd made it clear how they felt about Julie's lack of work-life balance. They didn't have time to drag her away from work and force her to relax. If Julie didn't want to make changes on her own, then Rae's hands were tied.

Rae checked the time and scanned the path that led to the parking lot. The team was finishing up their warm up, but there was no sign of Julie yet. They cast a questioning look to Beile who held up her phone and shrugged.

Irritation clawed at them, making them short-tempered. This was their second last practice before the Dragon Boat Festival regatta at the Toronto Islands. It was the biggest race of the year, and also, Rae's white whale. The Lavender Dragons had consistently come second and third place in their category year after year, but this time, Rae was determined to win gold.

They could do it. Rae could feel it in their bones. With Julie on the team, they'd been paddling faster and stronger than ever before. If they didn't win this year, it might never happen. But it would only work if Julie showed up.

Both Rae and Beile had called and texted multiple times, to no avail. The calls went to voicemail and the texts went unanswered. They couldn't wait any longer. They needed to get the team out onto the water. But even as everyone geared up and headed down to the dock, Rae's gaze kept drifting toward the clubhouse, hoping to catch sight of Julie with her bouncy ponytail jogging toward them.

Nothing.

Rae ordered everyone into the boat and they pushed away from the dock. They practiced their starts, timing, power rowing. With an uneven boat, everything was off, and they kept falling short of their targets. With each drill that didn't go according to plan, Rae grew more and more exasperated, infecting the rest of the team until everyone was grumpy and annoyed.

By the time they finished practice, everyone was ready to quit. As they headed back to shore, Beile shouted from her spot at the front of the boat. "Julie's here!"

As one, the entire team looked toward the dock where a single figure sat at the end, legs dangling in the water, watching them. Rae's anger exploded.

What fucking good was it for her to show up at the end of practice when they were already fucking finished?

Did she plan to run drills on her own? Had she shown up just to hang out afterward? And where the hell had she been anyway?

At the hospital, Rae was sure. And even though Rae had told themself again and again that they understood the importance of Julie's work, they couldn't help but resent all those needy mothers and babies right then.

They didn't speak as the team brought the boat alongside the dock, and one by one, each person climbed out. Julie stood off to the side, casting awkward smiles whenever someone glanced in her direction. She was still in her pink scrubs, feet bare, pant legs rolled up to her knees. Her arms were crossed protectively across her body, pushing her breasts up against the tight fabric of her shirt.

Rae hated that they noticed even when they were supposed to be angry with her. They also hated the surge of protectiveness they felt when they saw the dark circles under her eyes, the slump of her shoulders, and the overall sense of defeat radiating off her.

Wordlessly, Rae approached, stopping an arm's length away. They didn't trust themself not to pull Julie into a hug, rock her side-to-side, and tell her everything was okay.

"Sorry," she said, voice low like she was too tired to project any farther than the short distance between them.

"Work?"

Julie seemed to shrink even more. "Multi-car pileup on the Gardiner Express Way. One car held two friends, both pregnant. We lost one mother and baby. The other mom is in critical condition and her baby is in the NICU."

Rae recognized the way Julie spoke. The flat, deadpan tone made her sound like she was giving a book report rather than commenting on literal life and death. Rae felt like an asshole for being angry, for wanting Julie to be at practice rather than at the hospital. But their sense of shame didn't negate their anger. If anything, it amplified it.

Saving lives was important, obviously, but everyone in the boat had made a commitment to show up and work together. If Julie wasn't able to make dragon boat a priority, she shouldn't have agreed to join. It wasn't fair to Rae and the team. It wasn't fair to Julie either when she had to stretch herself so thin.

Julie scrubbed a hand over her face and turned away from Rae to look out over the water. "I, um..."

She sighed, and Rae gave in to the overwhelming urge to hold Julie. She clung to them, face buried in the crook of their neck, hands fisting the back of Rae's loose tank top. Her body shook in silent sobs, and Rae's heart broke for her.

How could she keep going on like this? Pouring herself into caring for others until she was wrung out and dried up? It wasn't even about dragon boat anymore. This had extended far beyond being chronically late and missing practices. Julie's inability to balance work with anything else was going to be her downfall.

"You're killing yourself like this," Rae murmured. "How much longer can you go on before you burn out?"

A wretched sound tore from Julie's throat, hitting Rae deep in their gut. Julie was hurting. Her single-minded devotion to her vocation was admirable. But what good was that if the job she loved put her into an early grave?

Remorse flooded through them, for all that Julie had sacrificed already, for the pain she was experiencing at the moment, for their own inability to do anything about it.

Their sense of protectiveness urged them to wrap Julie up and whisk her away to some place where the hospital would never find her, where her pager didn't work, and her cell phone had no service. Where no demands were ever made of her, and she could recuperate and heal.

This life she'd built was impressive, but it wasn't sustainable. Something had to give, and they were afraid it would end up being Julie herself.

"I know you love your job, babe, but there's got to be another way," Rae said, not caring if they sounded like they were pleading. They *were* pleading. They were falling in love with this woman, and they didn't want to see her be ground down into nothing.

The hollow sound of footsteps on the dock approached and Rae turned to find Beile standing a few feet away.

"Is she okay?" she asked quietly.

Rae responded with a grim expression.

Beile winced in solidarity. "Do you want to take her home?"

"Yeah, that's a good idea."

Together, Beile and Rae guided Julie back up the dock and toward the clubhouse. She didn't protest, leaning heavily on Rae, not watching where she was going. The team had already put away the equipment, and Rae held Julie while Beile grabbed their things for them and finished locking up. Then they carefully deposited Julie into the passenger seat of their car.

Shutting the passenger side door, Rae turned to Beile. "Good job today. Make sure everyone knows that."

Beile gave them a wry grin. "Because you were kind of an asshole during practice?"

Rae couldn't help looking contrite.

Beile gave them a soft punch on the arm. "Don't worry about it. We understand. I'll just tell them you're picking up the drink tab today."

"Great. Thanks," Rae responded flatly, rounding the hood of their car.

"Hey," Beile waited until Rae paused at the driver's side door and glanced up at them. "Take care of her."

Rae nodded. "I will."

SEVENTEEN

JULIE

JULIE STOOD across the street from St. Mitchell's hospital, and for the first time in her life, she didn't want to go inside. She'd never not wanted to go to work before. She'd never felt this heavy dread hanging around her neck, threatening to strangle her.

Yesterday had been one of the hardest days of her career. Her ward had already been at capacity with patients when the call came through about the multi-car accident on the Gardiner. There was no way she could have left her team to fend for themselves. But the entire time they were working on both mothers, she couldn't stop thinking about how she was missing dragon boat practice, how she was letting Rae down.

After Rae had driven her home, they'd fed her, put her to bed, and then stayed the night. She'd woken up this morning tucked in Rae's arms, and she hadn't wanted to get out of bed.

Julie never called in sick, but this morning, if Rae

hadn't needed to go check in on PoPo, Julie would have gladly written herself a doctor's note and stayed home.

Her phone buzzed, and Julie didn't need to check it to know it was the hospital. She was already thirty minutes late for the start of her shift.

She pushed down the dread, shoving it as deep inside as it could go, and forced herself to cross the street. The second she stepped onto her ward, it was go-go-go. Her brain kicked into overdrive, hyper focusing to keep her on task. There was no time for feelings, no space for fatigue. Just one patient after another for hours on end.

Julie felt like she was in a fugue state, operating on autopilot, her medical training taking over while her consciousness went into hibernation. When there was finally a moment of downtime, Julie found herself standing in the middle of a hallway, not entirely sure how she got there, or what she was supposed to do next.

Viola appeared in front of her, arms crossed, a worried expression on her face.

"What is it? Where do you need me?" Julie asked, mentally running through the list of patients that were currently admitted.

"Staff lounge. Now." Viola didn't wait for Julie to respond before turning on her heel and marching off.

Julie followed, confused but too tired to question Viola. She still wasn't fully present when they arrived and found Rae standing in the lounge, waiting for her.

"What are you doing here?" Julie asked. "I thought you were going to see PoPo."

Rae's lips twitched in a wry smile. "I did. I was there all morning."

Julie glanced at the clock on the wall, only then realizing how late it was. She was more than halfway through her shift, and she hadn't taken any breaks yet. But that didn't explain what Rae was doing here. "Oh. Uh..."

Rae pointed to the insulated bag sitting on the table in the corner. "I brought food. I figured you probably hadn't eaten yet."

"She hasn't," Viola piped in. "She's been on her feet since she walked in the door."

"There's plenty if you'd like some," Rae said to Viola.

Viola's eyes brightened. "Don't mind if I do."

Julie watched in stunned silence as Rae unpacked their bag, pulling out three plastic takeout containers.

"Ooo, where did you get this?" Viola asked as she cracked open the lid of one.

"I made it."

Viola paused, stunned. "You made it?"

"Yup." Rae opened another container, entirely nonplussed.

Mouth-watering aromas beckoned Julie closer. One container was filled with stir-fry rice noodles with egg, barbecue pork, and shrimp. Another contained tea eggs—eggs hard-boiled in black tea. The third held puffy white buns that were mostly likely filled with lotus seed paste. Julie stared in shock. She knew Rae could cook. She hadn't known that Rae could *cook* cook.

"Hurry up and eat. Before it gets too cold." Rae

portioned out the food and handed plates to Julie and Viola.

Viola didn't waste any time before digging in. "You better watch out," she said to Julie between bites. "If you don't lock this one down, I'm going to steal them from you."

Rae chuckled, and Julie smiled, the joke finally drawing her out of her trance.

"Thanks, Rae." She leaned in to give Rae a quick kiss on the cheek before she started to eat. Her stomach grumbled loudly, protesting how long it'd been ignored, and her eyes stung as gratitude swept through her.

She really didn't deserve Rae. Their thoughtfulness and generosity were overwhelming, especially when Julie was already stretched so thin. She sniffled, trying to hold back the tears. She couldn't break down, not now, not here. Not when she would be called back to work at any moment.

"I've been trying to get this one to take a vacation."

Julie snapped out of her daze at the comment to find both Rae and Viola watching her.

"She hasn't taken a vacation in all the time I've known her," Viola said, eyes still on Julie.

"Doctors get vacation days, right? They're not indentured servants or anything. They're allowed to take time off, aren't they?"

Viola laughed. "Yeah, they can take vacation. They can even take sabbaticals."

Rae perked up. "Oh, yeah? How does that work?"

"You have to have worked here for a certain amount

of time. Ten years, I think? Then they can take a month-long sabbatical."

Julie shook her head. She knew of other doctors who had done that, but it wouldn't work for her. "No, they have to be working on a research project or some sort of secondment with another hospital."

Viola scoffed. "Yeah, they've got *research projects* in *Fiji*."

"So she doesn't need to be working on research?" Rae asked, eyes narrowed in thought.

"Nope, not as far as I understand it."

"And how long have you been working here?"

Julie had to stop and think before she could answer Rae's question. How long *had* she been working here? So long she'd lost track. "Almost... eleven years."

Rae's eyebrows shot up. "So you qualify."

"No, I—I mean, I don't—" Julie sputtered, not knowing how to respond. Taking a sabbatical wasn't that easy. There were hoops to jump through, approvals to get. She didn't know the details, but it had to be a complicated process. She couldn't just take off for a month because she felt like it.

But before she could put up more of a protest, her pager went off. She jumped at the unexpected buzz against her hip, and her heart kicked into high gear. "It's the ER. They need me downstairs for a consult."

She looked up at Rae, bracing herself for their disapproval, apology poised on her tongue. But their expression was soft with understanding, if a bit resigned.

"Go. Be a doctor. Save some lives."

Julie's heart expanded to bursting with a plethora of feelings that were too big to contain. Gratitude. Admiration. Love.

So much love, springing up from the depths of her soul. More than she'd ever felt before. More than she thought was possible to feel. She loved Rae with everything she had and more.

But she had to go. There were patients waiting for her. She had responsibilities she had to fulfill.

She stood from her seat and leaned in to give Rae a kiss. She poured everything she felt into that kiss, repeating the three little words over and over in her mind. She hoped they could feel it. And if they couldn't, she would find a time to tell them.

When she finally broke the kiss, Rae's eyes were shining with affection, and she almost spilled the words right then and there.

"I don't know how long I'll be," she said instead.

"That's okay. I can meet you at home."

Julie's heart tripped over itself. Home. She liked the sound of that. Whether it was hers or Rae's, she didn't care. So long as they were together at the end of the day.

She nodded. "I'll call you when I'm done."

Then she turned and rushed out.

———

THE CONSULT in the ER turned into emergency surgery, so it was hours later before Julie was finally free. Rae was long gone by then, and even Viola had finished her shift. Julie dragged herself to the staff lounge and opened her locker. A sheaf of papers fell out and dropped to the floor.

Julie bent to pick them up, brows furrowing as she read the bright pink sticky note stuck to the first page. It was in Viola's handwriting.

———

JUST DO IT.

———

SHE PEELED the sticky note off and scanned the pages. It was a print out from the hospital's employee handbook, the policy for requesting sabbaticals. There was no mention of research projects. Nothing about getting seconded to other hospitals for cross-training or knowledge sharing. No requirement to attend conferences or pursue professional development.

There was a form she had to fill out. And she needed approval from her department head. Then file the form with human resources and... that appeared to be it. It looked too simple. Ten years of service for one month of paid time off? That sounded ludicrous.

And yet, it was all laid out there in black and white. A sabbatical. Julie could request one. Then she'd have one month to figure out what to do about the rest of her life.

EIGHTEEN

RAE

SITTING IN THE LIVING ROOM, Rae spotted Julie through the window as she came down the street. They'd left the hospital soon after Julie had gone back to work, and Julie had texted when she finished her shift. They stood and moved to the front door, opening it as Julie arrived.

She stepped through the door, dropped her bag on the floor, and grabbed Rae on both sides of their face, hauling them in for a hard kiss.

Startled, it took a second for Rae to kiss her back. They swung the door shut behind them and wrapped their arms around Julie's narrow waist. They had a teasing comment ready for when the kiss ended, but Julie beat them to the punch.

"I love you." Her voice was breathy, but her eyes were bright and clear.

The three little words slammed into Rae like a sledgehammer, expelling all the air from their lungs, but they could see the love shining unwaveringly in Julie's gaze.

"It's okay if you don't feel the same way. I know I've been a mess ever since we met, and I haven't given you many reasons to love me back. But I'm going to change. I want to change. You're right. I can't keep working like this. Viola gave me some more information about that whole sabbatical thing, and I'm going to try to do it and—"

Rae put a finger over her lips to stop her rant, their heart so full of love and tenderness for this woman that their chest hurt. "I love you too."

Julie's eyes widened as if that was the last thing she'd expected to hear. "You do?"

"Yes." Rae laughed, feeling lighter than they had in a long time. Of course they loved Julie. Why else would they have put up with all the tardiness and missed practices? Why else would they have gone out of their way to take care of her? To bring her food?

The answer was so obvious Rae was a little embarrassed they hadn't connected the dots sooner. But now that it was out in the open, it felt like everything they'd been through the past several months had been leading up to this moment.

"I do. For some time now, I think."

The smile on Julie's face was so dazzling, even the dark circles under her eyes and the lackluster pallor of her skin couldn't detract from it. Rae basked in its radiance and let it fill them up to overflowing.

"I don't deserve you," Julie said, her voice thick with emotion.

Rae's brows slammed together in indignation. "Why would you say that?" they asked even though they knew.

Julie didn't think she deserved anything good. She didn't think she was allowed to be soft or have needs. She thought she always had to be strong and rely on no one else but herself.

"Because I..." She trailed off, shaking her head. She stepped back from Rae and threw her hands helplessly in the air.

Rae grabbed them when they landed heavily on her thighs. "No," they said, cutting off whatever self-deprecating comment Julie was about to make. "This isn't about who deserves what. Love isn't a merit-based system. I love you because you're you—all the good and all the bad. You wouldn't be who you are without both."

Tears welled up in Julie's eyes, and a couple blinks had them spilling down her cheeks. Rae led Julie over to the couch in the living room and pulled her down so they could cradle her in their arms.

"But I'm such a mess," Julie protested, clinging to Rae.

"What's wrong with that?" Rae argued back. They knew what Julie was trying to get at, and they refused to give in to her flawed logic.

"Because it's—" She let out a frustrated sound that had Rae smiling despite themself.

"Because you've held yourself up to an impossibly

high standard that no one can meet, and now you're berating yourself because you're not superhuman."

Julie let out a soft huff of defeat.

"It's okay to be messy, babe. Everyone is messy." Rae rubbed their hand up and down Julie's back and she melted into their embrace.

They were silent for a few moments, taking comfort in each other's presence. Gradually, Julie's breathing evened out, and when Rae glanced down to where Julie's head was resting on their shoulder, she'd fallen asleep.

Carefully, Rae eased Julie down onto the couch and covered her with a blanket. Then they picked up their laptop and moved to the armchair to continue their research. They'd been looking up how doctors could start their own practices. What kind of licenses they needed to get, what kind of equipment they would need to stock. They'd even come across someone out in Ottawa who was retiring and looking to sell their practice along with their existing patient list.

Rae had no idea whether Julie would be open to owning her own practice. Certainly, it would be a lot of work, but then, being a business owner of any kind was a lot of work. Rae didn't know anything about medicine or running medical clinics, but they knew how to run a business, and whatever they didn't know, they could learn.

More importantly, though, having her own clinic would allow Julie to set her own hours. No more twelve-hour shifts that grew to fourteen, sixteen, or eighteen. No more being on call and getting dragged in whenever a critical patient took a turn for the worse. No more emergency medicine that took a toll on her emotions.

Julie stirred, rubbing her eyes with the heels of her hands, then pushing herself up with a groan. "I fell asleep?"

Rae closed their laptop and set it aside. "Yeah."

"Sorry." Julie sat up on the couch, blanket pooling in her lap. Her hair was in disarray, and a little bit of drool had dried at the corner of her mouth.

Rae's heart clenched with how much they loved this woman. This strong, beautiful, messy, flawed woman.

"Um, could you get my bag for me?" Julie asked, sheepish and adorable, pointing to her big canvas tote that still sat on the floor next to the door.

Rae rose to grab it and brought it over to Julie. They sat down next to her as she dug through the thing and pulled out a sheaf of papers.

"This is what Viola gave me," she explained, unfolding the papers and holding them out to Rae. "It's the hospital's sabbatical policy. According to that, it's a pretty simple process. I just need approval from the head of my department and submit a form to HR."

Rae flipped through the pages, giving them a cursory scan. A ball of nervousness formed in their stomach at what this meant. Could Julie actually be thinking about taking a sabbatical? Was she actually willing to step away from the hospital? "Oh yeah?"

"I, uh, I've already set up a meeting with my department head."

Rae glanced over at her, unable to suppress their surprise. "Really?"

Julie nodded. "It's on Monday."

It was almost too good to be true. Not only that this opportunity existed, but also that Julie was actively pursuing it. It wasn't a long-term solution. A month would go by pretty quickly, and then Julie would be right back where she started. But it was something. And it would give Julie time to explore other options.

"When would you want the sabbatical to start?" Rae asked, their nervousness mixing with excitement.

Julie shrugged. "I don't know. As soon as possible, I guess? It might take a week or so for them to rearrange schedules, and I'd have to hand off my patients to other doctors. Maybe two weeks at the most?"

Rae stuck the papers back into Julie's bag and moved the whole thing to the floor. They took Julie's hand and brought it up to their lips for a kiss. "That's great news, babe. I'm so proud of you."

A blush blossomed across Julie's cheeks, and she dropped her chin to her chest. "It's not anything to be proud of."

Rae put a finger under her chin and forced her to look up at them again. "It is. It's huge. Big changes are never easy, especially when they go against everything you've believed about yourself. I'm glad you're finally making yourself a priority."

Julie shook her head. "Not just me. Us. I'm making us a priority."

Rae's breath caught in their chest. They hadn't

wanted to ask too much of Julie too quickly. Her own well-being came first, then they could work out the kinks in their relationship. But seeing the sincerity in Julie's eyes, hope sprang from the deepest part of their soul.

They leaned in and gave Julie a kiss, pouring every ounce of love and devotion they felt for her into it. This could work. They would make it work. No matter what it took, Rae was all in.

"I love you," they murmured against her lips.

"I love you, too," she murmured back.

NINETEEN

JULIE

RACE DAY. The biggest dragon boat regatta of the season. The rest of the city was still asleep, but a crowd had gathered at the Jack Layton Ferry Terminal in downtown Toronto, all waiting for the first boat that would take them out to the Toronto Islands where the day full of races would take place.

The crowd was eerily quiet for its size, but underneath the early morning atmosphere was a hum of electricity bouncing from one person to the next to the next. Julie could feel it skitter across her skin, raising goosebumps along her arms.

It had been ages since she'd been to a regatta, and even longer since she'd raced in one. She was practically bouncing on her toes, her adrenaline levels through the roof, fueled not only by the energy all around her but also by the prospect of a future with Rae.

The meeting with her department head had been earlier in the week. She hadn't been thrilled with the idea of losing Julie for an entire month, arguing that this would set Julie back in her career. But Julie was adamant, and she eventually approved the request. They'd agreed on a start date, and now Julie only had two more shifts before she was free.

All because of Rae. Because Rae loved her. Because Rae had taken a chance on her.

She wasn't about to let them down.

The Lavender Dragons were in line to board the ferry with PoPo in her wheelchair leading the way. Julie and Rae had made an early morning pitstop at the long-term care home to spring PoPo from her room. Apparently, she came to the race every year, and she was the team's loudest cheerleader.

The line started to move, and Julie gave PoPo's shoulder a light squeeze. "Hang on. Here we go."

PoPo's eyes were bright with excitement as Julie pushed her wheelchair up the wide ramp and onto the boat. "Go to the front, I want to see where we're going!" PoPo demanded.

Obliging, Julie brought her through the length of the boat, all the way up to the front, and positioned the wheelchair right next to the railing. PoPo pushed herself to her feet much more quickly and smoothly than she would have before her hip surgery. That was one silver lining from the accident—all that physical therapy had made her stronger than she'd been before.

"PoPo, be careful!" Rae chided, hurrying up behind their grandmother, putting a protective arm around her waist.

PoPo tried to wave them away. "Aiya, I'm fine!"

"The boat is going to rock back and forth. It's dangerous to be standing, PoPo. You could fall again."

"I'll hold onto the railing! Julie, tell Rae to go away!"

"Nice try, PoPo, but that's not going to work. Julie knows I'm right."

Julie watched the two with a grin on her face. It warmed her heart to see them argue and banter, and when they dragged her into their little squabbles, Julie felt like she'd found the family she never knew she wanted.

"I think she'll be okay, babe," Julie said with an apologetic look. "I can stand behind her in case she stumbles, but I don't think the waves are very big."

PoPo looked triumphant. "See? I'll be fine. Julie said so."

Rae shot Julie a glare, but it didn't have any heat in it. "Traitor," they accused even as a smile tugged on their lips. Rae reached for her and pulled her into their arms with a growl. "You're supposed to be on my side."

"I am on your side," she replied, blinking innocently.

Rae grunted, narrowing their eyes suspiciously.

Julie's heart skipped a beat. She couldn't believe how much she loved them. She couldn't believe she was capable of so much love. It grew and expanded in her chest, spread to her extremities, and made her feel like she was exploding with joy.

The ride out to the Toronto Islands was only about fifteen minutes. Then another ten-minute stroll across the island to the race grounds. PoPo joined the other family and friends who had come to cheer for the Lavender Dragons, and a regatta volunteer directed the team to their designated prep area.

Spirits were high and the air thrummed with energy. Rae led them through a series of warm ups—a couple laps around a big field, jumping jacks, push-ups—then they called everyone into a huddle.

All eyes were fixed on Rae, whose eyes shone with ferocity and determination. They radiated command and control, and Julie couldn't help the swirl of arousal in her stomach.

"This is it!" they called out as everyone placed a hand into the middle of the circle. "Today is the day we've been training for. Months of hitting the gym. Hours on the water. It all boils down to the few minutes we have out on that course. We've done the work. We know how to win this thing. Trust the training. Trust each other. Victory, on three! One! Two! Three!"

"Victory!" Julie shouted as loud as she could, throwing her arm into the air and jumping up and down.

The team broke apart, and Rae gave each person a high five as they jogged out to the dock where their boat was already waiting. Julie was the last person in line, and instead of a high five, Rae hauled her in for a kiss.

Hard and quick, the kiss left Julie's head spinning and her whole body tingling.

"I love you," Rae said, adding to Julie's giddy feeling.

"I love you, too." Then she yelped at the slap Rae landed on her ass.

"Let's do this!"

They were the last two into the boat, and as soon as they were settled, the team pushed off the dock and paddled to the starting line. Julie gripped her paddle, taking several deep, calming breaths. No one in the boat spoke, everyone focused on the job they'd come here to do—paddle hard, win gold.

A whistle blew, and the team raised their paddles into the start position. A few seconds later, a gun sounded, and they were off.

All thoughts evaporated as adrenaline took over. The beat of Beile's drum reverberated through the boat, a single heartbeat tying them all together. It was all Julie could hear as she paddled—twisting as she reached forward, pulling with her whole body, remembering to breathe through the movement.

Water splashed on her face and swirled in the lake as the boat flew by. Faster and faster until everything was a blur of white.

Then suddenly it all stopped.

Julie blinked, and a second later, sounds came roaring back through her ears. It was a cacophony of noise that came from all directions, leaving her disoriented. Her lungs burned as they struggled to suck in more oxygen. Her limbs felt like jelly from the exertion. And for a few moments, Julie couldn't tell what was going on. What happened? Did they win?

There was a murmur at the front of the boat.

"I don't know!" Beile called out. "It was too close to call. They need to check the cameras."

Then moments later, cheers erupted from the stands.

All heads swiveled toward the shore, and Julie immediately spotted PoPo standing by a railing, both arms raised, waving mini-flags with the Lavender Dragons' logo. Her smile was pure joy. Around her, other friends and family of the team were going wild, jumping up and down and screaming at the tops of their lungs.

"Did we win?" Julie twisted in her seat to look back at Rae.

But Rae was glaring at PoPo. "What is she doing? She's not even holding on to anything."

Laughter bubbled out of Julie, effervescent and uncontainable. She reached for the back of Rae's neck with one hand and yanked them in for a kiss.

"We won!" she shouted.

It took a beat for Rae to register what she'd said, and Julie watched the transformation on their face.

"We won!" they roared, and the entire boat exploded in cheers.

Screaming and shouting, splashing each other with water, they paddled back toward the dock and scrambled out of the boat to give each other bone-crushing hugs. Julie got passed around from one team member to another before she finally found her way to Rae. Collapsing into their embrace, she felt like she would burst with happiness and love.

The rest of the morning was a whirlwind. They joined PoPo to watch a few more races, cheering on the other teams from Toronto. At the medal ceremony, Rae got a little teary-eyed when the race official placed the gold medallion around their neck. PoPo insisted on getting out of her wheelchair for photos with Julie and Rae.

Then, riding high from their win, the team descended upon the pop-up market next to the race grounds.

A stage had been set up with performances from local children's dance troupes, music acts, and martial arts demonstrations. Vendors sold Chinese-style art, jewelry, clothes, and other random knick-knacks. There were at least three bubble tea vendors and half a dozen food stalls selling grilled meat, shaved ice, and zongzi, the sticky rice dumplings wrapped in lotus leaf that were the main festival dish.

Rae pushed PoPo's wheelchair, the two of them bickering as Julie strolled next to them. They stopped at the edge of a circle to watch a dragon dance—a team of dancers lined up in a row, each holding poles attached to an oversized dragon puppet.

As they moved, the dragon circled and undulated like it was flying through the air. A small band with cymbals, drums, and gongs played a driving beat that grew faster and faster as the dragon danced. It was mesmerizing to watch.

The audience crowded in, pushing Julie into Rae, and they snaked an arm around her waist to pull her closer. She leaned into Rae' solid strength, skin slightly sticky from sweat, the scent mixing with hints of floral that always clung to Rae.

This was her life now—this could be her life forever. She didn't want to give this up for anything, not for her job at the hospital, not for advancements in her career, not for any kind of praise or prestige. None of that was more important than Rae and the love they shared.

The dance ended, and the audience dispersed. As they continued along the rows of vendors, Julie looped her arm through Rae's, savoring the closeness, the simple intimacy of claiming each other in public.

They stopped at a vendor selling zongzi, and Julie ordered three different flavors while Rae took PoPo to find an empty picnic table. It had been ages since Julie had had zongzi—usually she was so busy with work, she missed the Dragon Boat Festival altogether, never mind found time to go out and buy any of the lotus leaf-wrapped dumplings.

The first bite was heavenly. The sticky rice was flavored with savory, fragrant soy sauce, and the filling of pork, shiitake mushrooms, and egg yolk were perfectly umami. She ate silently as PoPo and Rae continued to squabble over which flavor was the best.

"When is your wedding?" PoPo asked out of the blue. "Don't decide on a date yet. I need to look at the fengshui charts to find an auspicious day."

Julie froze with her hand halfway to her mouth.

Rae rolled their eyes and groaned. "PoPo, don't start."

"Why not? You need to get married so I can meet my great-grandchildren!"

Julie choked on her own saliva.

"PoPo!"

"You're not getting any younger, you know," PoPo

said, expression smug. "And neither am I. I want to go to a wedding. I want to hold babies."

Rae dropped their face into their hand, and when Julie managed to shake off her shock, she reached over and pulled their hand away. She met their gaze and felt all the love they shared between them.

She didn't know when or whether they'd get married, or if they would have kids. She didn't even know what would happen in the next couple of months. But she did know one thing: no matter what happened, Rae was the only person in the world she would want by her side.

EPILOGUE

RAE

RAE WAS at the back of the store when the little bell on the front door rang.

"Welcome to The Flower Shoppe!" Raufikat called out. "Oh, hi Julie!"

Rae adjusted the last sprig of baby's breath in the bouquet they were making, then wiped their hands on their apron. A minute later, Julie appeared, and Rae had to remind themself how to breathe.

She had her hair down in glossy black waves, and underneath her oversized fall trench coat, she wore a form-fitting pencil skirt with an equally form-fitting turtle neck.

Rae had always liked the way Julie looked in her scrubs, but they had to admit, Julie's business professional look was next level hot. They opened their arms, and Julie stepped right into them. With her heels on, they were about the same height, perfect for kissing.

"Right on time," Rae murmured against her lips.

Julie smiled sheepishly. "I was hoping to get here thirty minutes ago."

Rae chuckled softly. Tardiness might always be Julie's downfall, but at least she'd found ways to try to compensate.

She'd really put in an effort when she went on her month-long sabbatical in the summer. And now, three months later, it was official—she was no longer an employee of St. Mitchell's Hospital. Instead, she'd signed on with a couple of clinics around the city, splitting her hours between them, and only going into the hospital when her patients were ready to deliver. It still meant she got called away at times, but it was nowhere near as bad as it was before.

"Just give me a minute to clean up," Rae said, reluctantly stepping away from Julie. They made quick work of cleaning up the scraps of leaves and flower stems, wiping up all the little puddles of water on the table. Then they hung up their apron and slipped out to the front where Raufikat was making the rounds with a watering can.

"We're heading out now. Need anything from me?"

"Nope. I'm all set! Have fun at your grandmother's birthday party."

"Thanks. Call me if anything comes up."

Julie had her head bowed over her phone when Rae returned, and they stifled a sigh. Expecting Julie not to work was like expecting her not to breathe.

They gathered up their things and picked up the

bouquet to carry out to the car. Julie followed, phone still in hand as she slipped into the passenger seat.

"How was your day?" Rae asked when they got on the road.

"It was great!" Julie said, lighting up with excitement. "I met with a lesbian couple who are interested in IVF, and guess what?" She didn't wait for Rae to answer. "They own a couple of coffee shops!"

Rae laughed at Julie's obsession with coffee. Ever since she moved into Rae's house last month, their kitchen had been overtaken by coffee paraphernalia. "Oh yeah? Are they going to give you discounts?"

Julie's expression grew mischievous. "Well, I mentioned I always wanted to open a coffee shop and remember how we joked about doing a joint flower and coffee thing?"

Rae did remember. It had been something Julie had tossed into the conversation early on, but Rae had never thought it would come to anything.

"Uh-huh," they said cautiously, not sure where this was going.

"Well, they think it's a great idea." Julie beamed at them.

Rae turned on their indicator light and waited until they finished the left turn before responding. "They did?"

"Yeah, they did." Julie reached across the center console and put a hand on Rae's thigh. They covered it with their own. "What do you think? Worth meeting with them and having a conversation?"

Rae gaped, not sure they fully understood what Julie was saying. "Wait. What?"

"It'll just be a get-to-know-you thing. Learn a bit more about how their business works and see if it might be something we're interested in."

"Uh..." Rae honestly didn't know if they were prepared to take on a massive project like that. Not when things with Julie were still settling into place. But then they snuck a quick look in Julie's direction, and the joy they saw in her eyes quashed any trace of doubt in their mind. "Yeah, sure, can't hurt to talk, right?"

"Exactly!" Julie picked up her phone again and started tapping away. "They said we can stop by their store next Monday. It's by the University of Toronto campus, and it's called School Grounds, isn't that cute?"

Rae chuckled softly and shook their head. They should've known Julie had already set up the meeting. "Very cute."

Twenty minutes later, Rae pulled into the parking lot of PoPo's long-term care home.

Inside was chaos. Every single resident had congregated in the home's large lounge area, which was decorated with balloons and streamers. A homemade sign hung on the wall, proclaiming "Happy 83rd Birthday!" Amber and the other home staff were laying out the catering on tables lining the far wall.

PoPo was the center of attention, preening as her friends fawned over her, but the second she spotted Rae and Julie, she shooed her friends away.

"My Rae of sunshine!"

Rae moved to bend down and give their grandmother a hug, but PoPo pushed herself to her feet instead. They bit back a grumble, reminding themself it was good for PoPo to be on her feet and active.

"Happy birthday, PoPo." They handed her the bouquet of flowers.

PoPo gave them a cursory glance, then looked past Rae to Julie. "Oh, thank you, Rae. Julie! Come and give me a hug!" PoPo practically pushed Rae out of the way to make room for Julie. Honestly, Rae couldn't blame her.

Laughing, they stepped back, overwhelmed with a sense of rightness as they watched Julie with PoPo. The two of them had grown close during Julie's sabbatical and now they regularly ganged up on Rae over all sorts of things. It was one of the best things they loved about their little family.

Their hand drifted to the small box in their pocket. They'd picked it up from the jeweler earlier in the day, and now they just needed to find the right time and place to pop the question.

Uncertainty and doubt had plagued so much of the start of their relationship, and there'd been so many times when Rae had been close to giving up. But they were glad they hadn't, that they'd had faith in the love they and Julie shared. Because now, they'd never been more certain about anything else: they were going to spend the rest of their life with Julie Chan.

ACKNOWLEDGMENTS

DRAGON BOATS & DOCTOR'S NOTES started out as a short story that appeared in a holidays anthology, but even after it was published and in the world, Julie and Rae never quite left me. I always felt like there could be more to their story. It took me a while and a lot of trial and error before I could figure out exactly what that story was.

I'm so glad I stuck with them and let them reveal their story to me in degrees. I truly believe that this novella has given them room to grow and develop into the characters they were always meant to be.

If you've enjoyed Julie and Rae's story, please tell your friends! You can also leave a review on Amazon, Goodreads, or your own social media profiles so that other lovers of sapphic romance can meet Julie and Rae too. 🤍

ABOUT THE AUTHOR

Hudson Lin was raised by conservative immigrant parents and grew up straddling two cultures with often times conflicting perspectives on life. Instead of conforming to either, she has sought to find a third way that brings together the positive elements of both.

Having spent much of her life on the outside looking in, Lin likes to write about outsiders who fight to carve out their place in society, and overcome everyday challenges to find love and happily ever afters. Her books are heartfelt, gritty romances featuring queer people of color.

Visit her website at HudsonLin.com.

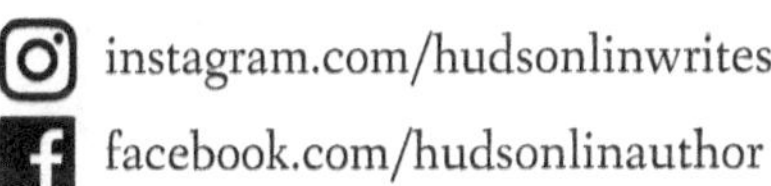

instagram.com/hudsonlinwrites

facebook.com/hudsonlinauthor

ALSO BY HUDSON LIN

Jade Harbour Capital Series

Hard Sell

Closing the Deal

Going Public

Stand-Alone Books

Dragon Boats & Doctor's Notes

Three Months to Forever

Inside Darkness

Stepping Out in Faith

Fly With Me

Lessons for a Lifetime

Coffee House Short Stories

Take Me Home

Ipso Facto ILU

My Name on Her Lips